If Ye Loathe Me

A.S.Chambers

This edition published in 2024.
First published 2022 by Basilisk Books
Copyright © 2024 Basilisk Books.

Cover art © 2022 Liam Shaw.

ISBN: 978-1-915679-37-6

Acknowledgements

Many thanks to the long-suffering artistic genius that is
Liam Shaw for his awesome artwork.
Thanks also to Fi for her proof-reading skills.

A special thank you to my following Book Club members
for their dedicated support:
Paul Lewis & Gemma Innes.

Also, a shout out to the following Kickstarter backers in
helping this book reach publication:
Simon Brindley, Debs McGowan, Ron Chick,
Lachlan Hardy, Robyn Lankston, Rebecca Armstrong,
Rohanna, Mike Armstrong, Nadine.

Also by A.S.Chambers

Sam Spallucci Series.
The Casebook of Sam Spallucci – 2012
Sam Spallucci: Ghosts From The Past – 2014
Sam Spallucci: Shadows of Lancaster – 2016
Sam Spallucci: The Case of The Belligerent Bard – 2016
Sam Spallucci: Dark Justice – 2018
Sam Spallucci: Troubled Souls – 2020
Sam Spallucci: Bloodline - Prologues & Epilogue – 2021
Sam Spallucci: Bloodline – 2021
Sam Spallucci: Fury of the Fallen – 2022
Sam Spallucci: The Case of The Pillaging Pirates – 2023
Sam Spallucci: Lux Æterna – Due 2024

Short Story Anthologies.
Oh Taste And See – 2014
All Things Dark And Dangerous – 2015
Let All Mortal Flesh – 2016
Mourning Has Broken – 2018
Hide Not Thou Thy Face – 2020
Out of the Depths – 2023
Hear My Scare – Due 2025

Ebook short stories.
High Moon - 2013
Girls Just Wanna Have Fun – 2013
Needs Must - 2019

Novellas.
Songbird – 2019
Bobby Normal and The Eternal Talisman – 2021
Bobby Normal and the Virtuous Man – 2021
Bobby Normal and the Children of Cain – 2022
Bobby Normal and the Children of Cain – 2022
Bobby Normal and The Fallen – 2023
Bobby Normal and the Black Dragon – 2024
Child of Light – Due 2024
Child of Fire – Due 2025

Omnibuses.
Children of Cain - 2019
Macabre Collection: Volume One – 2022
Macabre Collection: Volume Two – 2023
Sam Spallucci Omnibus: Volume One – 2022
Sam Spallucci Omnibus: Volume Two – 2024
The Adventures of Bobby Normal – 2024

Contents

How The Tibbles Got His Name

"It began when I was little… I was encouraged to go questing around the garden searching for ancient arte-facts that Daddy had hidden under a hedge somewhere. At first it was fun. Everything is when you're little, isn't it?"
Eloise Richmond - Fallen Angel

The sun beat down at the far end of the long, perfectly manicured garden, somewhere in the deepest depths of rural Oxfordshire. It was possibly the hottest day of the summer. Not that the small girl cared; she was on a mission.

No, not a mission. A *quest*.

She flumped herself down under a large tree, taking advantage of the handy shade, and rummaged around in her quest bag. In reality, it was a *Barbie* shoulder bag that Lisa Mulgrew's mother had bought her for her fourth birthday, but Ellie had taken a black Sharpie marker to the picture of the doll figure. She had scribbled a helmet over the iconic toy's blonde locks and had added a long sword in the doll's hand.

Ellie was attired in a similar fashion, with a

homemade helmet fashioned from aluminium foil perched atop her blonde locks with their unusual red streaks. It went perfectly with the small plastic sword that she had tucked through the belt of her battered, muddy trousers.

That was how girls were *supposed* to look. At least in Ellie's opinion.

Most of the other girls she knew thought differently. Well, their mums seemed to, anyway. When she had turned up at Maisie Runcorn's birthday party, it had been fancy dress, so she had insisted on going dressed as the Green Knight from the bedtime story that Daddy had been reading her. She had thought that the costume she had made had been awesome! She had taken loads of old cardboard boxes, decorated them with bright green paint and attached masses of green strips of paper to them in order to make her rustle as she moved. She had even spoken in a big deep voice all the way through the party, just like the knight in the story. However, when it had reached halfway through the party, it had become apparent that none of the other mums (who had dressed their daughters as princesses and fairies) were letting their children play with her, she had asked Daddy to take her home early. Maisie's mum had asked Daddy why they were leaving early and he had said something loud which had made her mouth open in a big, shocked oval shape.

Daddy did that to people he didn't like.

Daddy did that a lot.

It made Ellie smile.

Sometimes, if it wasn't past her bedtime, she would sit curled up on the sofa with Mummy and watch Daddy on the big television in the living room. There were two types of programmes that he appeared in. There were the ones where he was walking around faraway places, talking about the people who had lived there thousands of years ago. He would inform the viewer clearly, precisely and with a great deal of passion about how these people had lived, what they had believed in and how they had died. Ellie's favourite show like this was the one with the big brick buildings in the very hot country. Daddy worked there a lot and she wanted to visit it sometime. Perhaps when she was a grownup.

The other type of programme that Daddy appeared on would be one in a studio where he had to sit and talk with other people who weren't as clever as him. Ellie would get very excited as she watched Daddy's eyebrows rise up like they always did when he thought someone was being very silly indeed. Then he would say words that sounded very intelligent and whoever the silly person was would be left unable to talk back, their mouth open like Maisie Runcorn's mum's. Sometimes, when Daddy thought the people that he was on telly with were "beyond stupidity", he would even get up and walk off while they were still filming.

Ellie dug into her quest bag and pulled out the piece of parchment upon which Daddy had written her latest quest. It had very precise instructions. She was to go down to the end of the garden and, under the large oak tree, she was to survey her surroundings until she located the red banner in the nearby undergrowth. When she had found the banner, she was to dig with her trowel and find the special talisman that she needed to collect. It would help her on her next quest.

The four-year-old pushed back her aluminium foil helmet and lifted her hand above her eyes in an attempt to keep out the glare of the sun. From the shade of the oak tree, she let her eyes track around the hedge at the perimeter of the garden. The banner had to be there somewhere, but she couldn't see it. Perhaps it had fallen over?

She fished a peanut butter and jam sandwich out of her quest bag and chewed thoughtfully on the wholemeal bread. Daddy had been in a bit of a hurry today. His latest book was due out next week; the one with the large picture of the Grail on the front. This was why she was off pursuing her quest on her own while he was sat in his office shouting funny words at his printer. Normally he would be here as her steward, helping her on her way. Perhaps, when he had placed the banner, he had not forced it deep enough into the ground and it had fallen over?

Ellie nodded as she stashed half of the uneaten sandwich away for later (it always paid to conserve rations). She would just have to walk carefully along the edge of the hedge until she located the banner. It would be there somewhere. Heaving herself up and slinging her quest bag over her shoulder, she began to examine the base of the hedgerow, methodically lifting the overhanging branches with the tip of her sword.

It wasn't long before she found the small red banner. However, it wasn't planted in the ground as it should have been. Instead, it was gripped firmly in the mouth of a diminutive brown dog.

The small girl frowned. This was an unexpected problem. She knew that you had to be careful around dogs. They could either be very friendly or rather bitey. Judging from the size of this one, if it turned out to be the bitey sort, it wouldn't actually do much damage, plus as it sat there with the banner in its mouth, the small dog was wagging its little tail, which suggested that it might be friendly. Not taking her eyes off the dog, she set her bag down and drew out the remains of her sandwich, tore it in half and offered a piece to the tiny banner snatcher. The dog cocked its head, stood up and wandered over. Dropping the banner at her feet, it whisked the sandwich out of her hand and wolfed it down in one whole lump.

Ellie giggled. "Well, I guess you must be hungry," she said to the dog. She tore the remnant of her snack into two more pieces, ate one herself and offered the rest to the little canine, which gratefully accepted the treat.

Ellie knelt down on the grass and examined the dog. It was indeed very small and a light brown in colour. Its hair was incredibly short and it looked like it would die from the cold if it spent too much time outside. Also, it wasn't wearing a collar. "Do you have a name?" she asked him.

The dog sat on its small haunches and once again cocked its head, causing its ears to flop over in an inquisitive manner.

"Apparently not," Ellie surmised. "I think you really ought to have one," she said. "Everyone has a name. Mine is Ellie. Well, that's the short version, anyway. Mummy and Daddy only tend to use my full version if I'm in trouble." She frowned as she thought hard about the little dog.

And as she thought, she felt her brain go warm, as it did sometimes. Warm and fuzzy.

It didn't do that a lot, but when it did, unusual things happened. Like when she had gotten into trouble in her first week at school. The teacher's special pen for writing on the big computer screen had gone missing. The woman had been convinced that one of the class had picked it up and taken it. Now, she had been speaking all happy and jolly, suggesting that it wasn't something to worry about too much and that whoever had taken it had obviously done so by mistake. However, even though she had said that if that child was to own up and bring it back now they wouldn't get into trouble, Ellie had known otherwise. She had felt her brain go warm and fuzzy and she could hear nasty words in the woman's head, saying things that she would like to do to them when she caught the little thief. Then, Ellie's brain had gotten even warmer and, on a television screen in her head, she had seen her teacher's hands opening the top drawer to her desk and putting the special pen in there. So, not wanting the teacher to be cross, Ellie had put her hand up and told her where it was. Again, the teacher had *appeared* to be happy, but Ellie's warm fuzziness had shown her that she was, in fact, really cross for being made a fool of by a four-year-old. Not only that, but the teacher had used her full name.

So, after that, whenever Ellie's brain got warm and fuzzy, she imagined that she was pouring a bucket of ice-cold water over it to cool it down. As a result, the fuzziness was happening less and less.

Which Ellie considered to be a very good thing indeed.

This time, the fuzziness was concentrating on the little dog. Ellie frowned. She guessed that it couldn't do much harm to see what happened, so she closed her eyes and let the warmth wash over her. A curious noise filled the ears inside of her head. It was like a bunch of sparrows chittering in the trees on a warm summer night. It was a soothing and pleasant song and there was the light fluttering of wings mixed in with the melody.

Her eyes reopened and the little dog was still sat

there, intently watching her.

"I think I'll call you Mister Tibbles," she said.

Mister Tibbles barked, apparently loving his new name.

Ellie smiled. "Okay, now we've got that sorted, Mister Tibbles, could you please show me where you got that banner from?" She picked up the little flag and showed it to the dog who first ran around her feet in a happy circle before bouncing off to a piece of dark soil under the hedge. He began to scrabble at the disturbed earth and Ellie pulled out her trowel, joining him in his excavation. "Wait a minute!" she protested. "You'll disrupt the site."

Mister Tibbles sat back and looked at her with complete canine incomprehension.

Ellie pulled out four tent pegs and a ball of twine as she explained to her new friend. "Daddy does this for a living. He goes all over the world digging up old things. He says you have to be very careful and note everything down as you go." She pulled out her notepad and carefully wrote down in what a four-year-old took for meticulous handwriting: *site under hedge, dug a bit by dog.* Then fished out her ruler and measured carefully before pegging out an exact square around where Tibbles had been digging. "Right, *now* we can begin," and with her trowel, she carefully scooped up handfuls of loose earth, placing them in precise piles to one side. "We have to be able to put them back afterwards," she explained.

It wasn't long before her trowel hit something hard. She noted in her book: *item just under surface.*

Tibbles stood next to her, his tail wagging excitedly as she pulled a small, roughly shaped piece of wood out of the ground. Ellie wiped the loose soil off its surface and noted a decoration that had been carved into it: a goblet and a sword.

"Wow! It's the Grail and Excalibur," she explained to the dog. "That makes it incredibly special. They're what Daddy says other people call *archetypes*. But he thinks they're real and one day he'll find them."

The little dog whimpered.

Eloise frowned. "What? What's the matter?"

Mister Tibbles lowered his muzzle to the floor, his thin tail immobile.

"Are you scared?" the worried girl asked, and she reached out to stroke him.

As her small fingers touched his light fur, everything changed…

…Everywhere was white. It felt like it should be a large room, but there were no walls. All that she saw were two things hanging up in the air: a Cup and a Blade. She stood gazing up at them and, in her ears, she could hear a three-fold rhythm, it pounded deep down into her heart. There were footsteps and she was aware of a figure walking towards her. He was dressed in the purest white; six long wings spread out to his sides. With eyes that burnt like suns, he gazed upon her. He pointed up with a finger that was enveloped in fire towards the Cup and the Blade and intoned in a voice older than time:

"We are one…"

* * *

As the woman bent down to pick up the artefact, not a crease formed in her smart green, two-piece suit. "She looks so peaceful," she commented to Mister Tibbles as she let her fingers stroke a lock of the red colouration in the otherwise blonde locks of the small girl who slept peacefully next to the disturbed earth.

The dog shimmered and changed in shape as he took the form of the small angelic winged creature that he really was. Sophia heard his chittering voice of concern.

She shook her head. "No, she'll be fine. She'll just sleep it off. She'll have no memory of this for now and her powers will subside until she really needs them."

Again, the small creature chittered.

Sophia raised an eyebrow behind her severe glasses. "What a stupid question that is," she laughed. "Of course I'm sure. I mean, she is *me*, after all."

Tibbles shrugged, then his eyes snapped up to the far end of the garden, up by the sprawling country pile as they heard a deep, masculine voice call out, "Eloise! Eloise Richmond! Where are you?" The Dominion looked up and couldn't help but notice a tear forming in his companion's eye. He tugged at her skirt.

"I know," she said, "We had better go. But," she gestured to the wooden token, "I'm taking this wretched thing with me." Looking at the carving of the Cup and the Blade, she muttered. "We need to work out how it ends up in *his* hands. If we can, we might save so many lives."

And, with that, they faded away into nothing, as if they had never been there, leaving behind a sleeping four-year-old who dreamt of a world of knights and quests and of a dragon so powerful that one day, in the far distant future, it would make the whole world tremble at its roar.

6:25

He woke up.

Howard Maitland's weary grey eyes cranked themselves open, begrudgingly permitting him enough light with which to observe the flashing time on the clock radio: 6:25.

Another day.

For one blissful moment, he lay perfectly still, peacefully cocooned in the fresh white handspun bedlinen that he and his wife of five years, Tabitha, had bought on impulse whilst honeymooning down on the Dorset coast. As his memory recalled the knowing smiles of the elderly shopkeeper, he ran his usual morning mental checklist of his extremities: flexing fingers, wriggling toes, rolling shoulders. When he was ready to put them into action, he heaved himself around and up into a sitting position.

"Morning, Darling," came the voice of his wife of five wonderful years.

Howard smiled to himself and felt the mattress undulate slightly as she too sat up.

He turned round to face...

...not his wife.

The creature was unlike anything he had ever seen before. Its blackish-brown skin seemed to shimmer in the light of his wife's bedside light. Drops of moisture glistened on its hard, alien surface. Its wrinkled eyelids blinked slowly and the pale white orbs beneath them gazed blindly in his general direction. It opened its mouth to speak and jagged, irregular fangs framed a slithering green tongue.

"What's the matter, Darling? Are you okay?"

Howard opened his mouth in an attempt to scream, but there was no air, just suffocating deadness. He gasped and gagged as the creature that had most certainly not lain with him on the sandy beach at Weymouth leant forwards, a clawed hand reaching out for his cheek. Desperately, he writhed and wriggled in an attempt to free himself as the claws reached down and grabbed at his shoulder. He felt their hard edges dig into his soft flesh, scrape at his skin.

And still he could not scream; could not breathe.

"Howard! Howard! What's wrong?"

Howard snatched in a gasp of hot air as his head snapped away from the pillow. His whole body whipped and cracked in an erratic movement as he felt himself twist up in the duvet, almost rolling off the side of the bed in the night-time dark.

"Howard?" came Tabitha's voice once again as she clicked on her bedside lamp. "It's okay. You were having a nightmare."

He felt his racing heart pounding in his chest and his stomach was lurching in his middle.

"Nightmare?"

The beautiful woman who had held his hand as

they had paddled through warm water on the southern coast nodded. "You'd just gone to sleep."

Howard glanced at the clock: 12:05. She was right. "Sorry," he mumbled. "Did I disturb you?"

She shook her head. "No, it's okay. The storm was keeping me awake anyway."

Howard frowned. "Storm?"

"Can't you hear it?"

All he could hear now was his thumping heartbeat. "No. Sorry."

"Look, why don't you have some sleeping pills? I've got some here. They'll help you sleep."

Howard glanced down at the three small pills in her hand. They were the same shade of green as her eyes. "No. I'll be okay. Like you said, it was just a stupid dream."

"You sure?"

He looked down at the pills again. He hated taking pills. "No. I'll be okay." Then, after plumping up his pillow, he settled his head down and closed his eyes.

He woke up...

His eyes snapped open. 6:25 read the clock radio. There was an immediate tension to his chest as he recalled the nightmare, the obscene creature in his marital bed.

Just a dream: he reassured himself but, all the same, he slowly reached his hand behind him and let it feel the warmth of a soft human butt through a smooth satin nightdress.

Howard nodded to himself and rolled over to see the brown hair of his wife on her pillow as she kept on sleeping. He allowed himself a contented smile before he pulled himself out of bed and padded down the landing towards the bathroom.

After performing the morning *essentials*, he washed his hands and splashed cold water on his face. It was an important day today. There was a meeting at work for which he had to look decidedly spick and span. His up-and-coming company, which were becoming well known on the international stage for producing all manner of boxes, were launching a brand new range of reinforced corrugated cartons that could catapult them into the big league.

Howard stared morosely in the medicine cabinet's mirrored surface. Right now he was decidedly neither spickish nor spanish. He ran his fingers through his matted bed hair and sighed. He needed to pull himself together right away and get sorted.

Teeth first.

He took the orange toothbrush from the glass on the side of the vanity unit and squeezed out a pea-sized blob of toothpaste onto the worn bristles then began to scrub away. It was as he dug around his rear teeth that something struck him.

Why wasn't he using the electric toothbrush?

With the brush clamped between his teeth, he looked across the surface of the vanity unit for the all-singing and all-dancing bit of kit that they had bought just last year after the bathroom had been modernised.

It wasn't there.

Neither was the electric socket that had been installed during the redecorating.

Howard frowned as he felt something that definitely wasn't enriched with sodium fluoride start to squirm around inside his mouth. He screamed in surprise and disgust as he spat out the brush. It landed on the floor in a gob of spit and paste. His stomach lurched as he bent down to inspect it. The head of the brush was writhing back and forth of its own volition. He knelt on the expensive laminate that had come highly recommended from the specialist installer in town and touched the worn bristles with a good amount of apprehension. They fell away, disintegrating to a nothingness, leaving just a broken, jagged end. Carefully, he picked up the handle of the brush, stood up and peered down in gruesome fascination as small, white insects spurted out of the fractured plastic, scurrying away across the polished laminate flooring on minuscule, rhythmic legs.

"Are you okay, Darling? I heard you shouting."

He spun around to see his wife stood in the doorway, her sleepy eyes half-closed.

"The toothbrush..." he held up the broken handle, the insects still spilling out and down onto the bathroom floor. "Is it... Is it *supposed* to do this?"

His wife opened her eyes.

Her pale, dead eyes.

She smiled.

Crooked white fangs crept out beyond her parted gnarled lips.

Howard screamed as he lunged forward and jammed the snapped end of the toothbrush into her cheek and twisted the impromptu weapon. The creature's fallacy dropped and once more it was there in all its vibrant hideousness; its blackish-brown and callused skin slippery to Howard's touch as it glistened in the light from the bright, modern lamp that was set flush in the ceiling.

Its hand reached up and grabbed him by the throat, a crushing grip squeezing into his windpipe.

He sat bolt upright gasping for air, his hands scrabbling at his unimpeded throat.

"Darling, it's okay. It's just another dream."

Howard's head snapped to his right and saw his wife sat there next to him. "*Another* dream?" He looked back to the clock radio: 12:06. He'd been asleep for just a minute. It had felt so much longer.

"Come on, settle down," his wife soothed, her gentle, warm hands easing him back down into the soft, handspun cotton. "Look, please have some sleeping pills. This storm is playing havoc with your nerves."

Howard glanced once more at the three green pills in her hand. The pills that were the same colour as her eyes. "I can't hear a storm," he whispered.

"Darling, it's been raging all night. I think next door have even lost a couple of slates; it made a hell of a racket. Please, have the pills. Get some good sleep. You'll feel better in the morning."

He shook his head. "No. It was just a bad dream."

"You want to talk about it?"

He thought about plunging the broken toothbrush into his wife's cheek. "Not really."

He lay his head down on his pillow and closed his eyes once more.

He woke up...

Cautiously, Howard opened his eyes. 6:25.

His hand reached out behind him.

Wife's butt.

So far, so good.

He eased himself out of bed and wandered down the landing towards the bathroom on which they had spent a reasonable amount of money the year before. There, in its rightful place on the vanity unit, sat their electric toothbrush, plugged into its socket, fully charged and ready to be used.

He realised that he hadn't actually breathed until this moment.

Howard smiled and began to get ready for work. He had an important meeting this morning about a new line of reinforced packaging that would revolutionise international shipping. He had to look his best and be on top form. The small up-and-coming company for which he worked was depending on him.

An hour later and he was cruising down the A6. The motorway was shut due to flooding from the storm and he was having to take this alternate route. Fortunately, he was ahead of the crowd and the traffic was almost non-existent, so he was able to put his pedal to the floor and gun the Merc, his pride and joy, down the open road.

He was just coming into civilisation when his phone began to ring. Checking the display, he saw it was his wife and clicked on the hands-free. "Hi. What's up?"

"Just checking you're okay. I didn't get to see you before you headed out."

"Yeah. I didn't want to disturb you. You know, what with all those dreams last night."

There was a pause on the other end.

"Dreams?"

"You know. Just after we went to bed."

"Darling, I don't know what you mean."

"The storm. It kept waking me up."

"I... I really don't know..."

Howard peered out of the windscreen and frowned. The sky had turned a curious shade of green. The clouds seemed to be whirling misty strands down towards the town below.

"I woke up twice, I think it was..." he began, but was cut short as something smashed against his bonnet, bounced up into his windscreen and catapulted over onto the road.

Howard, slammed on his brakes, stopping blindly, unable to see through the crazed glass. He lurched out of the door and pulled himself forwards towards the crumpled mass of white that lay broken by the side of the road. Nausea rose in his throat as he recognised the flowery pattern on the nightdress and the brown hair through which blood was now oozing.

It couldn't be.

How could it be?

She was on the phone, just now.

He staggered over to the crumpled body of his dead wife and carefully rolled it over onto its back.

The creature that wore his wife's nightwear opened its death white eyes and snarled through its jagged teeth as its powerful hand snaked its taloned fingers around Howard's neck.

"Jesus!" he yelled as he snapped awake, his heart ramming against his chest and bile gathering in his throat. He lurched from his marital bed and ran to the bathroom which had cost so much money to decorate, lifted the lid of the toilet and was promptly sick. He was flushing the contents of his stomach away when his wife walked in, concern in her deep green eyes.

"Darling, whatever's the matter? Have you had another nightmare?"

Howard couldn't speak. All his nerves were on edge and his stomach was rolling like a sailing ship in a typhoon. It took all his effort just to manage a single, nervous nod.

"Come on," she soothed. "Let's get you sorted. It's this damn storm."

He nodded as she carefully sponged his face, even though he couldn't hear the storm above the beating of his frantic heart. He just let her clean him up and lead him back into the bedroom. 12:07 read the clock radio.

He climbed back into bed after his loving wife, his darling Tabitha, had straightened out the expensive hand-spun cotton sheets, purchased five years ago on their Dorset honeymoon. He lay down as she stroked his tousled hair, concern in her beautiful green eyes.

"Here, Darling. Take these."

Howard just stared at the three pills that were the same shade of green as her eyes.

He shook his head. "No," he muttered. "I think I'll be sick if I do. I'll... I'll just go to sleep."

He closed his eyes.

He woke up...
6:25.
He reached behind him.
Nothing. No one.
He stretched out further.
The other side of his marital bed was empty.

Howard sat up and pulled himself out from under the expensive handspun sheets. He walked over to the window and drew back the curtains. Eerie green clouds billowed up above and a raging storm howled through the early morning. He watched enrapt as snaking twists of va-pour dragged themselves away from the writhing emerald sky to the streets down below.

There was a noise.

From within the house.

It was rhythmic, like the slow breathing of a predator lying in wait.

Howard turned and crept carefully out of the bedroom, not turning on any lights. He let the rich pile of the landing carpet muffle his footsteps as he made his way to the bathroom which had cost an arm and a leg to redecorate last year.

The bathroom door was at the end of the landing, opposite him, and it was through this that he could see the creature, silhouetted against the unnatural light of the green storm which edged its way through the frosted bathroom window. The beast had its back to him and its arms were raised towards the olivine light, its clawed hands beckoning the weird weather down to the earth.

Something primal leapt up from inside the mild-mannered box salesman and he charged down the landing towards the monster, screaming with all his pent up rage as he did so. He threw himself at its wet, glistening back and rammed it down, clashing its head against the side of the fashionable enamelled bath, stunning the beast. He wrapped his fingers around the hard flesh of its throat and began to squeeze.

The creature thrashed around beneath him as it tried to escape, but Howard just laughed maniacally as he felt its larynx crush under his grip. The monster's mouth snapped open and shut as sounds tried to make their way, plaintively from between its snaggly fangs. Howard took one of his hands and forced it over the monster's mouth, stifling the cries for freedom.

He felt the jaw working hard under his grip as he pressed down.

He felt the hard, wet skin.

He felt the human teeth.

He felt the soft, feminine skin.

He saw the shocked green eyes.

He snapped backwards and threw himself off his terrified wife's flailing form. She sputtered and coughed as she forced herself to breathe, her hands gripping the expensive handspun linen of their marital bed.

"Oh, God! Oh, God!" Howard wept as he staggered around the room, pulling at his hair. "What have I done?"

Tabitha shook her head, coughed and beckoned to him. "Just... a... nightmare..." she finally managed.

He crawled across the bed and curled up, trembling, in her arms. "I'm so, so sorry," he cried into her soft brown hair. "I'm so... so..."

She shook her head. "Not your fault. See. I'm okay." She pulled away and smiled at him, her green eyes shimmering in the vague light. "Let's settle you down."

Howard nodded. "I think... I think I'll have those pills now."

He looked down at the pills that shimmered in the same green as his wife's eyes and took them from her outstretched hand. He downed them with a swig of water from the glass on his bedside.

Just before he drifted off to sleep, he saw that the clock radio read 12:08.

He woke up...

There was a mechanical hum as the mechanism of the stasis chamber began to wind down.

Howard took a deep breath as he opened his eyes. The timer above him read 6:25. He hadn't even been under for six and a half minutes.

The lid to the chamber popped open and he eased

himself up and out into the brightness of the clinically white room.

"Well?" Tactician Sherbourne asked. "How did it go?"

Tactician Howard Maitland shook his head. "The entity was too strong. We vastly underestimated its psychic abilities. Every time I came close to destroying its higher functions, it forced me out with images from my subconscious. Eventually, it just wore my reality down." He headed over to the wall of the lab. "Show," his tired voice commanded to the controls.

The substance of the wall altered into a vast view screen of the city outside. From the depths of ominous green thunderheads, gigantic swirls of mist were circling down onto the buildings and streets below. Beneath them stood a gigantic beast, its black-brown skin glistening in the moisture of the encircling storm. Its cruel claws were raised in a summoning plea to the mist, controlling its direction and an eerie howl was emanating from between its jagged fangs. As if sensing that it was being observed, it turned towards Maitland, its dead white eyes staring straight at the tactician, and smiled.

Awakening

At first, they thought it was the military; some new sort of weapon designed to destroy their houses, their family homes, in a quicker, more efficient manner. They ran out into the streets, screaming and shouting in anger and surprise as floors shook and plaster crumbled from walls. Some grabbed weapons; others were armed with just their ire and fear.

But, as they congregated in the dusty streets, in the light of the day, they spied no jet planes streaking overhead, they heard no rattling of gunfire. It soon became apparent to all that this had been no tactical strike designed to drive them from their homeland, but something from deep beneath the ground upon which their families had dwelt for generation upon generation.

As most stood in bewildered huddles, trying to comprehend what had occurred, others on the outskirts of the settlement let out a cry of discovery. The villagers scurried through the narrow streets. They came to where a great chasm had appeared below a cliff next to a dried-up river that had once brought nutrients to their crops before it had been dammed by those who wanted power for their sprawling, modern cities. They stood upon the edge of the precipice, unsure as a body as to what they should do. Old men muttered about places of danger and women held their young ones close. Eventually, five young men grabbed a length of rope, tied it to a nearby tree and ventured down into the gloom.

The old men said that they would not return.

The women's children began to weep.

For what seemed like the span of aeons, there was silence. Not a sound could be heard from the depths of the hole. No one could make out any flicker of light from the young men's torches. They were soon considered lost, dead.

But then, from out of the depths came a jubilant cry.

"We are rich! We are rich!"

The men knew what they had to do as soon as they found the stone door. One immediately clambered back up the side of the exposed cave to start ringing around all his usual contacts. Three others returned to their homes to fetch their usual excavation equipment: spades, picks, crowbars and props.

One, the youngest, agreed to stay behind to watch over their precious discovery.

As he sat there in the silence of the half-light, his entire world illuminated by just a small torch, he studied the stone door that had caused so much excitement and which promised wealth beyond their imagination.

Pictures had been worked into the portal's surface, not just light etchings like a lover would scrape in the bark of an olive tree, but raised, enduring carvings that were designed to remain through the terrible ages that would pass as empires rose and fell; a testament to a story from thousands of years previous.

At the apex of the door stood a huge building. It was constructed out of cyclopean stonework with bricks larger than the average man. Around its base were worshippers, bent in supplication and prayer. There were men, women, children, all seemingly enthralled by whatever the building represented or, perhaps, what it contained.

But these were not the only characters in the ornate bas relief. Around the edge of the picture were creatures the like of which the young man had never witnessed before. They were tall and powerful, possessing no neck but instead a dome-like head that seemed to be one with their torso. Their long arms stretched beyond all proportion as they appeared to work in innumerate teams, dragging the large blocks of stone to the temple before placing each brick into its precise position. The boy watched the story unfold, as the creatures seemed to rise up from the very earth itself. They were obviously not human. Were they the djinn of old?

But what was apparent was that they were slaves. There, standing proud in elegant, flowing robes was a man with a stern and handsome look to his face. He was posed with an arm outstretched, pointing towards the temple and, around his neck, he was adorned with an amulet that contained a round, polished stone. This stone captivated the attention of the young man as it bore the only colour on the whole carving.

It was a vivid green — not the living, verdant green of a plant or a tree, but a bright, artificial hue of something unnatural, not of this world. From its core, tendrils of what appeared to be smoke emanated out towards the enslaved supernatural workers, as if breathing life into their lungs.

The youth blinked and screwed up his eyes as the half-light appeared to play tricks with his vision. It seemed to him that the strands of vapour were swaying and eddying on the surface of the stonework, twisting and undulating as if they were alive. Fascinated, he let his inquisitive fingers trace along the lines of mist until their tips reached the round stone itself. There, in the depths of the cold earth, he discerned the vaguest of sounds, a whisper. His head snapped back to the opening above, convinced that it must be his friends returning, but there was nothing. His eyes refocussed on the mysterious stone and his trembling fingertips brushed its smooth surface once more. Again, the distant noise appeared from nowhere in his ears, calling just to him; crying out, desperate to be heard — like a small child that was lost in the dark.

His lips were suddenly parched and he ran a nervous tongue across them. His fingers began to lovingly caress the image of the green stone as the small childlike voice started to whisper secret promises to him and him alone. It told him that he should take the stone and hold it in his grasp; feel its unimaginable power coursing through his palm into his body. It told him that it had so many secrets that it wished to reveal. There were so many wonderful games that they could play. It would show him how he could harness the creatures that rose from the earth, how they could march across the face of the planet, doing his bidding. They were its playthings, its toys. They could be his too, all he had to do was reach beyond this door, into its prison, and pick it up.

They would have so much fun together.

The young man was aware that he had stopped breathing and, as he let out a breath in the still, cold cave, his ears heard an unfamiliar word slide across his tongue in his own language: "Constructs."

"What did you say?"

The youth screamed in terror at the sound of his companion's voice. His friend laughed as the others clambered back down the rope with their assortment of tools.

"Let's get this open," the friend said.

The young men were skilled in what they did. There was a great deal of money in providing antiquities for private collectors; there was a *fortune* made by providing them *intact*.

It took more than a week to get the huge stone sentinel out of its resting place. For four of them, this was of no concern. They knew that they already had buyers lined up for whatever lay inside the room beyond, so time and care were essential to preserve the integrity of absolutely everything and maintain if not increase its monetary value. Items of historic interest that were dug up in one piece gave the seller far greater bargaining power.

The youngest of the group, however, was considerably more impatient. With each strike of the pick, with each creak of the crowbar, the susurration in his head grew in intensity. Over and over, the small voice described the inordinate wonders that it would let him behold. Again and again he heard the marching feet of the army of constructs that would be at his command.

The stone in the bas relief yearned to see the light of day. He could feel its excitement brewing, its dormant power waking as it realised now that its escape from its sepulchral prison was imminent. There were times, times when the youth felt that he was tripping over into the realm of insanity, that he thought the entity in the stone walked alongside him in the cave, unseen by the other looters. Every now and then, he caught a glimpse of movement in the corner of his eye. There would be a flash of bright green hair and a white dress before the patter of small feet snatched the vision from his peripheral vision. Sometimes, in the deepest parts of the gloom, peering out of the depths, he was sure that he could see a pair of green, glowing eyes that watched their work with an insatiable hunger and excitement, but then he would blink and there would be nothing, just the small voice growing ever louder in his head. It spoke of how it wanted to once more feel the fresh air of the world above ground. It yearned to be reunited with its twin from which it had been separated after the temple in the carvings had been constructed. Together they would herald in a new era and he would be instrumental in this change.

"Show me," the young man demanded in his head. "Show me the future."

He watched vivid images in his head of streets flashing past him as he ran in a helter-skelter manner, his lungs afire with effort. They were the streets of Jerusalem that he knew well, had walked along so many times before. People backed away from him in obvious terror. There were gunshots from behind as soldiers chased him, but their aim was not true and they kept missing. Then, as he stood in the centre of the city, at the point where millennia ago creatures of clay had forged a great temple, he screamed to Heaven above and pushed down on a small device in his hand before there was an all-consuming blinding flash. He felt his spirit soar up into the ether and, as he looked down upon the world that he had just departed, he witnessed the rise of a huge mushroom cloud as all that existed for miles around was obliterated in a nuclear wasteland.

A shout of joy in the gloom of the cave dragged him back to the here and now.

His eyes widened as he watched the stone door prised from its centuries-old location. Songs of ecstasy resonated through his mind as he lay his eyes upon that which had been calling to him. There, in the middle of a small antechamber sat a small altar, plain in its appearance and upon it, cradled in a silken throne lay a hemispherical green stone. He pushed through his companions and grabbed the stone up into his hands. Ignoring their protests, he felt the power of the artefact coursing through his entire being. Its joy was incalculable, immeasurable.

It was free.

He looked down at the fear in his friends' faces as he opened his mouth and spoke words that came from within the green hemisphere: "We are one!"

And that was when the rattling song of gunfire filled the cave.

His four friends dropped instantly as the military men abseiled down into the depths, bright beams of light from their headpieces illuminating the gloom and efficiently picking out their targets. The youth dropped to his knees, cradling his precious treasure. Cowering in the dirt, he heard rather than saw the pair of confident feet that walked up to him.

"I believe you have something that I need," came a crisp British voice.

The youngster looked up and saw a man in his late thirties. He had blonde hair and bright blue eyes which were fixed on the green stone.

"It is mine," the boy wept. "It chose me."

"Really? Prove it."

The boy felt sweat, slick in his scalp. He swallowed and held up the stone. In his mind he saw legions of constructs rising from the earth to do his bidding, to strike this intruder down, but in his ears he heard nothing.

The man shook his head and simply plucked the stone from the boy's unbelieving hands as a child would take an olive from a tree. "Power craves power," the stranger explained, turning the stone over in his hands, examining it as one would a prize fish that one has just caught in the river, "and I can give this little one so much more than you are able to."

The boy watched as green tendrils of smoke began to effuse their way out from the stone and twine their way around the man's wrist before sinking down into his skin. The man groaned in pleasure and nodded in satisfaction.

He turned and nodded to one of his soldiers who snapped to attention, "Yes, Mister Stone."

The soldier aimed his weapon at the boy and a gunshot echoed around the cave.

Let Sleeping Dragons Lie

2:47.

His eyes stared at the digital clock radio. Sighing, he forced his eyelids shut and prayed for sleep.

3:05.

Was that all? Eighteen minutes? Just eighteen stupid minutes? He slammed his head into his thin, worn pillow and groaned.

3:26.

He'd had enough.

Grunting, yawning, stretching, he swung his flabby legs out from under his sweat-stained bed sheets and sat for a moment on the edge of the bed.

The man ran his fingers through his lank, dark hair. Had he been dreaming? He was sure he had been dreaming.

Again.

The visit to the therapist...

...the dead therapist...

...had not solved his problems. It had been up to him to work them out on his own. So he had gone to a stupid self-help group where a group of *Me, Me, Mes* had treated it like some sort of non-virtual TikTok room, ensuring that they had been the sole centre of attention for a few seconds each.

Pointless.

So, he had gone to a bar. There had been a woman. Something had happened. He bit down on a chipped, cracked fingernail as he tried to remember what. They had been talking then it had been incredibly hot and he had been elsewhere, watching something. A fire? A blazing fire?

He shook his head. He couldn't recall, not properly. Everything was so vague, so fuzzy right now.

Like the dream through which he had just staggered.

There had been people in his dream. As he pulled on his sweat pants and slipped into a threadbare charity shop jumper, he definitely remembered people. They had all been sat around him: watching, listening. The flames of a crude campfire had flickered in their dark eyes, given an expectant glow to their faces as they had hung on his every word. They were people who were truly living with life and death problems, not like the little parakeets at the self-help group, completely obsessed with their pathetic sparkling reflections.

He paused halfway down the stairs of his tired suburban house. What had he been telling his audience? He was sure that he had been angry, but about what...? He frowned, dug deep into his subconscious, but it just wouldn't come. It was a greased marble that slipped casually out of his grasping fingers.

He made his way downstairs, into the cluttered living room that smelt of sweat, stale beer and takeaway pizza. He flicked on the television and frowned. It was running a newsflash of some sort. Something catastrophic had occurred somewhere and the newscaster was wittering on about people turning into wolves then dropping down dead. The man shook his head and switched the goggle box off. There would be no escape from insomnia here with stupid social media fake news like that.

Instead, he grabbed the brown padded jacket that he kept hung on the end of the bannister and slipped it on, before pulling a battered pair of old, comfortable Nikes onto his aching feet.

If only he could remember the details of the dream. He was sure it would help.

His key slid into the lock of his front door and he stopped, frozen.

He had not been alone in the dream. Someone had been next to him.

Who?

He scanned his eyes around his vague memory and saw nothing but an anthropomorphic blur; light at the top, darker further down. There was movement in the area that should have been a face. Fuzzed out lips were talking, the head shifting in a somewhat insistent, concerned manner. But all he could hear was an incoherent mumbling.

He shook his head and left the house, walking out into the cool, late January night.

Perhaps the fresh air would help.

Frost crunched under his trainers. It was a reassuringly real noise: tangible. The man enjoyed the feel of his feet treading one after another as he made his way to the park that was situated near his house.

He liked to walk. It was his favourite mode of transport. There was nothing to go wrong, was there? Bikes got flats; cars endured countless traffic jams; trains suffered numerous delays; planes plummeted from the sky, spiralling down to their doom, wings twisted and aflame.

The man lurched to a stop, his stomach knotted inside his gut.

That was dark. Where the hell had that come from, the image of burnt, twisted wings?

Not a plane.

He straightened himself up, drew a breath and entered the silent park.

He needed a clear head; not more conundrums, not more nightmares.

"Give us your wallet and your phone."

The man stood still. He was deep in the heart of the park, sentinel trees towering up around him into the indigo sky. He had thought that he was alone with his thoughts and his elusive dreams.

He had obviously been wrong.

There were three of them. He reckoned they were no more than twenty years' old each. Incredibly young. The one who had spoken was holding a knife, a pathetic little blade. He had seen knives much more deadly than this little toothpick before now. Knives and vicious blades that had been truly made to kill and maim rather than cause a mild inconvenience.

He frowned.

Where had he seen them?

His dream edged back into his mind. The people in front of him were holding knives, but they were fashioned from stone, not metal. It made no sense.

"Hey, I'm talking to you."

He snapped back to the here and now. The youth with the tiny little weapon had taken a step forward and was waving his pride and joy around with a puffed-up frantic vigour.

"Give us your stuff."

The man shook his head. "That's a pathetic little thing."

There was silence as the youth realised that he had just been verbally bitch-slapped.

"I mean, really, you and your buddies come out here in the middle of the night with that tiny little piece of scrap metal and you think the world is at your feet? Really?" The man felt the world around him glaze over as he continued. "You truly have no idea. If you had seen what I had seen, you would be curled up at home, not *in* your beds, but *under* your beds. Your Pokémon pyjamas would be wrung wet with your terrified urine and you would be screaming incoherently, your tiny minds unable to conceive what they had witnessed.

"I... I have seen civilisations rise and fall. I have *created* civilisations, put people on the right track, giving them the ability to grow and destroy all those around them. I have seen my people bathe in the blood of their enemies and rejoice in bacchanalian dances whilst all around them lies waste.

"I have seen a time when all you tiny little people will be nothing. You shall be hunted down, consumed and eradicated from the face of this planet. A power shall rise, the like of which your weak leaders will not be able to contain. His obsidian wings shall envelop the planet, causing the life force of the sun to diminish and your crops to fail. He shall drag you down into the mire of poverty, of serfdom and eradicate your vaunted sciences. His creatures shall stride unstoppable across the scorched land, disposing of your saviours and putting your pathetic little remnant to the torch."

His words ground to a halt and he was aware that he had reached out and grabbed the youth by the hand. His fingers gripped the youngster's hand tight around his knife and squeezed.

But, not with pressure. With heat.

The youth tried desperately to pull away, first terror consuming him and then searing pain as he felt the skin on his palm start to pucker and blister in an impossible heat. His panicked eyes flicked from his mutilated hand to the eyes of this crazed attacker.

And then he began to scream, for all he saw in the man's eye sockets was pure, inextinguishable flame.

"No."

The word was plain, calm and the man felt a gentle hand fall on his tensed shoulder. His grip slackened and he released his would-be mugger.

The owner of the word stepped forward. She wore dark hair tied neatly above her head, her clothes pristine, immaculate. "You never saw this," she said to the youths. "You were fooling around with a lighter and your hand got burnt," she instructed the lad in a firm, clear voice. "Now go. Never come back to this place."

The three boys gawped up at her, confusion in their eyes, then turned and fled out of the park.

The woman turned to the man. She placed a warm hand on his cheek, lifted his face so that her bespectacled eyes could gaze upon him, and smiled sadly.

"Who are you?" he asked.

The air around the woman seemed to coalesce into

a fog and her skin rippled as if it were water. Then, there in front of him, she changed into a woman with long blonde hair darted with red streaks.

He recalled the figure from his most recent dream and the mist from his memory dissipated, revealing the same form.

The woman from his dreams, the ones that had sent him to the useless shrink.

"Oh, my dearest love," she sighed, "what has happened to you?"

She was real.

She was real.

She was real.

The girl he had told the therapist about was actually stood here in front of him. She looked somewhat older, but there was no mistaking that distinctive hair. He reached up with a hand that had almost incinerated his mugger and playfully stroked her red streaks.

"They always fascinated you," she smiled, her face bringing welcome illumination to the gloom of the night.

"What is happening to me?"

The woman took a steadying breath as she tried to think of the best explanation. "You," she eventually said, "have been asleep a very, *very* long time. You tried to put right something that went wrong but things just didn't go as we had planned."

"What was I supposed to do?"

The woman placed her hand against the side of his head and looked deep into his eyes. He was stood in another place, the place of his dreams. In front of him, villagers dressed in an assortment of skins were watching him as he demonstrated how to sharpen raw flint into a wickedly cruel blade. They crowded around as he bound the stone to a long pole. They marvelled as he flung the spear, the beginning of a new age, and it harpooned a running animal.

The villagers learnt quickly and fashioned their own weapons under his watchful eye.

By his side, in the distant prehistoric past, his blonde-haired companion asked, "Are you sure about this?"

He breathed in the pure, unpolluted air and nodded. "It is the right thing to do," he reassured her "They need to be able to fight."

"How can that be?" he asked of her in the here and now. "That, that was..."

"A very long time ago."

"Am I waking up?"

"*When dragons walk the earth then all creation shall tremble,*" she recited, her face full of sadness.

The man flinched as something immense and brutal began to claw its way into his subconscious.

The woman blanched. "No, no, no. Leave it. You are not ready for that."

He shook his head as if to clear cobwebs that were settled across his synapses, deadening his senses, and when he looked at her again, his eyes were like fiery suns.

And he could see the beast standing before him in what appeared to be a church.

The creature was enormous, towering above all those who cowered away from its sevenfold gaze. The scarlet-scaled dragon roared in fury, its seven heads snaking this way and that, as if it was driven by an insurmountable rage that boiled deep inside its guts. The man looked down from his point of view and saw, in his hand, a sword that gleamed with the purest of light. He shook his head to clear his thoughts, rolling his neck as he did so. He felt his hair brush against something to his side and glanced at his shoulder. Was that a wing? A huge black wing?

The dragon roared once more and the man/angel lifted the sword high to challenge the beast who stepped forward, swiping out with a powerful claw. The man/angel screamed in a tongue that was as far from human as the edge of the solar system is from its star, and lunged into battle.

The man frowned. "What is this? What am I see-ing? What does it mean?"

"It means, my love, that it is not yet time for you to awaken from your slumber. The Divergence is close, but things are not yet ready and I cannot lose you again."

"I... I don't understand you..."

The man felt the earth shift underneath his feet and in his hands he held a round green stone. It was the most incredible thing he had ever laid eyes on. It was warm, alive. He could hear it whispering beguilingly in his head, trying to convince him that he was worthy of all its power.

He grasped the green artefact in his fiery hands and twisted, aware of someone screaming in furious rage as the stone snapped and was cleft in two, tumbling to the ground. A sallow-skinned man clothed in flowing dark robes lunged forward and tried to snatch them up but he let a stream of fire shoot out from his right hand, causing the would-be thief to dodge awkwardly and grab just one half of the stone before vanishing into thin air. He turned to his side and saw a teenage boy with dark wavy hair and blue eyes. The youth's mouth was moving as words formed on his lips, but the man did not hear them as he was deafened with joy.

"Alec…" he cried into the night air. "My son." Then, as more memories began to click into place like a child's sliding puzzle, "Amanda?" He grabbed the woman's arms. "Our children?"

She frowned. "There is so much I want to tell you… Alec is well, safe. I have met him. Amanda… I do not know."

He felt tears welling up in his eyes. "We must find her. We must! They took them!"

Tears tinged with scarlet were running down the woman's face. "We will, my love. We will. But not now. Now you must sleep once more."

He shook his head. "No! No! I cannot, will not. It is a hell, a living hell. I am me but not me. I cannot go back in that prison."

"You have endured so much worse," she wept.

And he knew that she was right. He felt the aeons of falling, of plummeting endlessly through the fiery waters, his skin scorched and his wings broken, bent.

And he remembered the name of the one responsible.

"Asmodeus," he growled. His fingers clenched and his hands became balls of pure fire. As his true form started to reassert itself.

The woman grabbed his shoulders as the incandescent fire began to spread up his arms. "No," she repeated. "Not now. You must sleep once more. If you wake, it will be the end."

He felt sudden calm ease its way into his limbs as he gazed upon her steady blue eyes with the tiniest of flames in the dark pupils. He remembered a bed where he had held her, loved her. He recalled the soft touch of her hand upon his cheek and her carefree laughter on a spring morning. He was aware of it cocooning him, swaddling him in a warm blanket, tucking him into his childhood bed where there would be no monsters waiting and he closed his eyes, ready for a dreamless slumber.

As sleep enfolded him in its tender arms, his lips released just one word: "Eloise."

The man opened his eyes.

4:37.

Had he been dreaming? He could not recall.

He closed his eyes once more and slept peacefully.

It was not yet time to wake up.

Priorities

As he wrenched the blade out of the guts of his former boss, Howard suddenly remembered that he would have to pick up a pint of milk on the way home.

Relics

It was warm. Blissfully warm. Stretching her long, smooth legs out under the sheer material of her flowing robes, she could feel the soft caress of the sun on her silken skin. Slowly opening her dark eyes, eyes that had witnessed the birth of the Physical Realm, she gazed down upon the throng of worshippers that knelt in supplication at her feet — praying to her, adoring her, chanting her name.

A contented smile touched her rouged lips.

This was the life.

Placing her hands on the arms of her highly ornate gold throne, she pulled herself up and watched as the devotees all fell on their faces, not daring to cast their unworthy eyes upon their goddess.

"I am going for a walk," she informed them in their language. "I am not to be disturbed."

The cowering devotees parted like water as she stepped down off the dais and glided out of the sanctuary. As the sun continued to beam down on her own little patch of self-made paradise, she let her bare feet guide her around to the back of the compound, her perfectly manicured toes relishing the crunch of fine, white sand beneath them. She entered the holiest place on the *bamot* and ran her smooth fingertips over the tall wooden poles that stood within her still, silent sacred grove. Each one was intricately decorated with pictograms and icons that spoke of her story, telling how she had arrived at this place and brought with her the priceless gift of civilisation.

Her hand rested on the reconstruction of one particular story. The pictograms first showed a barren wilderness, a desolate land untouched by civilisation. Then there was a stylised reproduction of her striding across the arid sand, water pooling where she trod. Next, plants grew from the nourished ground, providing all manner of vegetation. The peoples cultivated crops and they feasted. They fashioned a gold throne for her and worshipped her. Then, on her instruction, they cut down the seven tallest trees and brought them here to her *bamot*, where they would stand to tell of the wonders that their goddess performed.

She made to pull her hand away but found that she could not move. Staring in fascination at the pole, she observed that tendrils of small, olive green vines had snaked their way out of its surface and had wrapped themselves around her hand, first lithely twisting around her slender fingers, then leaping up and grasping at her wrist. Try as she may, she could not pull free.

There was a noise, a rustle and she felt more vines lash out from other poles, grabbing at her wrists, and also her ankles. She yanked and tugged, but the treacherous poles would not release her. They held her fast, a prisoner, just as *they* had been for so many years, here in her grove.

Then she heard the rumble like an oncoming

storm. Turning her head out across the blue ocean, she witnessed the waves rise up as one, a towering tsunami above the island, rolling in as if they were a wheeled army of Hittites or Mitanni. She opened her mouth to cry out, to stop them, but a treacherous branch whipped around her mouth as a gag, stifling her cry.

Then the wave struck, obliterating all that she had created and nourished, grinding it into a wet paste under the relentless force of the water. She stared in horror as the wreckage drifted aimlessly up past her to the distant surface of the inky waters, leaving her tied, trapped far down below in the bottom of the murky depths. She made to call out, to cry to the water, to tell it to stop, but she had no voice. No words could come from her mouth as she was not in possession of any breath. A searing heat was coiled dragon-like in her lungs and invisible weights hung on her limbs, making it impossible to move.

Panic began to rise in her chest.

She had been here before, time after time, this hellish place.

She knew what was to come.

She was not alone. There were others down here sharing the gloom of these dreadful depths.

They came now, both of them — their pale, bloated forms drifting through the watery half-light. The fallen goddess struggled again to break free, but it was no good. Like every time before, she was unable to escape as the dead, decaying bodies of her former lovers drifted into view before embracing her with their lifeless, rotting limbs.

Asherah awoke, screaming.

The expensive white linen was screwed up around her lithe body which was coated in the sweat of sheer terror. She sat shivering as she commanded the panic within her to subside. She would not be controlled by an infuriating nightmare.

A grunt of vague disturbance came from the other side of the bed. She looked down at the young boy in his early twenties and rolled her eyes. What the hell was she doing? Another in the latest line of conquests to try and distract her from the inevitable conclusion.

After god alone knew how many thousands of years of wandering this pitiful planet, she was bored. She cast her dark eyes around the hotel suite as her heart slowed to a more acceptable pace. The room was the height of luxury. Whatever the guest wanted, they had to hand: a well-stocked bar, a circular bath in which one could probably fit an entire football team, a wall of aired wardrobes to protect your finest clothes from even the tiniest of creases.

The vast majority of the planet's population could never even dream of the life that she led.

Yet, it was not enough. It was *never* enough.

Deep inside of her, as she walked this turgid planet for millennia after dreadful millennia, the hole, no the *chasm*, inside of her grew larger and larger. Soon, there would be nothing left of her, just the overwhelming sensation that she had had enough.

"You never realised just how good you had it, did you?"

She rubbed a stray tear away with an annoyed flick of a finger as she recalled *his* words. They had been stood at the feet of the grand steps up to the Temple in Jerusalem as the last construct had inserted the final stone. She and Asmodeus had been smiling to themselves, so proud of their little plan, so smug, and he had just turned to them and planted those seeds of doubt in their hearts.

How it had all quickly unravelled after that.

That was the past. She must not dwell on it.

The bedside radio declared that it was just after ten in the morning. How had she slept in so late? She never used to do that.

She needed a distraction.

She needed retail therapy.

The clothes were all very *nice*. Asherah ran her fingers over the supposed variety of fabrics that were, in reality, all the same cheap rubbish, and sighed. When had fashions become so dull? She appreciated that manufacturers had to make things that people wanted to buy, but couldn't they try and persuade the general public to push their tiresome boundaries at least once in a while? All the tops for women were described as "slouch tops" or "comfort fit". Whatever happened to the "Look at me and weep at what you cannot touch fit"?

She supposed that there would be better ranges in the larger cities, but here she was stuck in a small market town in the East Midlands. Why on earth had she decided to come here? She didn't have a clue. One day she had just found herself pulling off the A45 and driving up into the car park of Wellington University. That was where she had met the boy. He had been bent over inside the window of his car, fishing out a folder or something that he needed for a lecture.

Asherah had always been a sucker for a nice rear and he had never made it to the lecture. That had been two weeks ago and here she was, still here. At least she had *one* devoted worshipper who hung on her every word.

Just like Wallace had.

Well, that had been a right royal fuck up, hadn't it? Just like her long term on off *tolerance* of Asmodeus. Whenever he turned up, trouble always followed, just like it had last week. Asherah closed her eyes as she saw the burning wreckage of a car wrapped around a tree just a few streets away. At first it had felt like a fun distraction, but then...

"Do you see anything you like?"

Asherah was drawn from her reverie. She opened her eyes, turned and peered over the top of her dark glasses. The shop assistant was about her height, slim, blonde hair and blue eyes. Her figure made the most of an incredibly dull, utilitarian uniform.

"Why, I think I do," she smiled, then began to hum softly and slowly under her breath.

The woman gasped and swallowed as her pupils widened.

Asherah let the volume and intensity of her siren song increase as she drew closer to the subject of her attention. She stood so close that she could feel the heat of the human radiating out from her aroused body. The woman was panting heavily, gripping a clothes stand with one hand to steady herself. She closed her eyes and whimpered as the fallen angel ran a manicured nail down her cheek.

"Seriously? A shop assistant? And in Primark of all places?"

Ash's song abruptly ground to a halt as she turned and glowered at the intruder. He was nonchalantly rummaging through a selection of sports bras.

"I don't really think I can see you wearing these,

you know." Then to the flustered woman he snapped, "Get lost and don't come back."

The poor shop assistant straightened her clothes and scurried away.

"What do you want?" Ash sighed as she turned to walk out of the shop.

Asmodeus fell in step behind her. "Oh, just thought I'd drop by and see how you were doing?"

She snorted her derision as she glanced at him. He was still going with the black and moody fashion sense he'd been sporting since the nineteen-eighties. "A social visit? Really? How quaint."

They stepped out into the pedestrian precinct that made up the centre of the town. All around, people scurried about their business unaware that a pair of self-styled deities walked amongst them.

"It's getting worse."

Asherah turned to her on-off companion of the long, long millennia. "What is?"

"All this," he gestured to the shoppers and workers. "What the hell went wrong?"

"They outgrew us."

"Ungrateful bastards."

"That's the way it goes."

"We ought to change it."

"Really? And how would we do that? Set up some sweet little reality TV show? Perhaps have members of the public sat at home watching us go about our daily routine? We could call it *Gogglegods*."

"Not really what I had in mind."

"Oh, do share then."

"You *know* what I have in mind."

This gave Asherah pause. "Really? After all this

time?"

Asmodeus nodded. "This planet needs it. Look at what it's become. It has atrophied, limped its way into stagnation. It is quietly, placidly crawling into a dark corner readying itself to die in obscurity. It could have been so much more."

"It's not our world anymore."

"But it could be. All we have to do is use *it*."

Fire burned briefly in the female angel's pupils. "You know we can't. The moment you connect with *it*, *he* will know and he will come for us."

Asmodeus made a derisive noise. "You seriously still think he's around?"

"He's *always* around."

"I've seen neither hide nor hair of him since the Temple. He's long gone."

Asherah chewed her bottom lip. She wasn't convinced. "I don't know. Just because you can't see him, doesn't mean he isn't here."

Asmodeus shook his head. "Will you listen to yourself? What happened to you? When did you become so tame, so *vanilla*? You used to have the world at your feet, quite literally. Civilisations bowed down to you and adored you as their goddess. Hellfire! You single-handedly obliterated the Bloodline in Egypt. Troy was *razed to the ground* because of you! Don't you want that again? You know how good it felt."

She looked around the dull, grey people and imagined them all before her, bowing down, singing hymns, praying to her. Then the nightmare edged back into her head, and she felt invisible branches lashed around her wrists as the crushing water fell upon her. Something was coming, something immense and destructive. It would pay to be prepared.

She nodded to her old partner in crime. "I'm in."

Asmodeus grinned, snapped his fingers and they were elsewhere.

"Well, this sucks."

Asmodeus nodded in a reluctant form of agreement. "I agree that the place has certainly gone downhill since we were last here."

Asherah walked over to the scorched remains of what she presumed used to be a house. She ran her fingers over the crumbling brick wall and it disintegrated in her fingers. Looking up and down the main street, she could see instantly that the rest of the village was in a similar state of disrepair.

There was not a single sound to be heard.

She could taste the deaths of its inhabitants in the air.

"It's a morgue," she muttered. "Something happened here." She knelt down on one knee and held a hand out to the dusty earth, her fingers splayed wide. Asmodeus watched in silence as she concentrated on what lay down in the ground. As her pupils burned bright with fire, scant droplets of moisture rose from the parched ground and danced around her fingertips. She lifted the hand to her mouth and let the water settle on her tongue. Tasting of the precious, life-giving liquid, she said, "This happened months ago, towards the end of the summer last year. There has been no human interaction since then."

"What do you think happened?"

She stood up, reached out and a fine mist of vapour emanated from her hands, cleaning every trace of dirt off her tight, red leather trousers. "Do you not read the news? This area is a powder keg. Some government official probably decided that they wanted the locals out so they could build a factory here or something." She shook her head as she looked around the devastated village. At least when she had ruled here, there had always been a true purpose behind any destruction. It had been to punish those who spoke out of turn or no longer amused her, not just for the manufacturing of mass-produced pap. "Come on. Let's get your *toy*."

It was when they reached the outskirts of the village that they realised that the destruction may not have been brought about by a need to evict the former residents.

"I don't remember that being there," Ash said as she looked down at a wide rift in the land at the bottom of a cliff face.

"That's because it wasn't," Asmodeus frowned. "We buried the shrine deep down so it wouldn't be disturbed."

"Guess we didn't know much about tectonics back then."

Asmodeus swore as the air cracked and he vanished. Asherah counted to five and, bang on cue, there was an irate scream from the bottom of the chasm.

"They stole it! They bloody well stole it!"

"Of course they did," she muttered under her breath and transported herself down to see just how bad things actually were.

They were, it appeared, very bad indeed.

In the light provided by the glowing electricity that flickered around Asmodeus' hand, she could see that someone had done a right royal number on his tedious little shrine. The stone door had been pried opened and smashed, the insides ransacked. For once in his existence, her companion had actually put some care into his handiwork, rather than getting someone else to use their lifelong skills before being paid in an excruciating electrocution. He had carved ornate glyphs into the stone which had illustrated the building of the Temple. She had remembered his standing back and giving what was an incredibly rare thing for him, a contented smile of happiness, as he surveyed his handiwork. He had gone on to fashion a simple altar upon which he had reverentially placed his prized creation.

"The Potency has gone," he wailed, kneeling in the dirt and grasping at his hair. "How? How could this have happened?"

Ash glanced around at the patches of crimson that stained the floor and the walls. "With quite a bit of bloodshed, by the looks of it. I don't think up top was cleared out to be redeveloped. I think it was slaughtered to keep it quiet."

"*Him!*" Asmodeus glowered, the sparks of energy from his hands increasing, "*He* did this!"

Ash shook her head. "No. Not his style. He would have just walked in, taken it and gone. You know he has a soft spot for humans. He wouldn't have massacred them."

"Then who?"

Asherah pulled her companion to his feet and for once in over two thousand years, the hopelessness in his eyes actually made her feel sorry for him. "I don't know," she said. "But what I *do* know, is that we need a drink. A strong one, at that."

"What the hell is this stuff?" the despondent male

fallen angel grimaced as he knocked back his umpteenth shot of the clear liquid. "It tastes like horse piss. There's no fish in it, is there? You know I'm allergic to fish."

Ash smirked around a matching grimace as she followed suit. They had relocated to somewhere slightly more salubrious. They had both decided that they couldn't be bothered with the bright lights and luxury of a big city, so had settled for a small bar just a few miles from where the Potency had been hidden for two and a half millennia before someone unknown had found it, grabbed it and slaughtered everyone in its proximity to keep them quiet of the fact. Sure, it was a complete dive bar: the upholstery, that there was, on the furniture was tattered and worn; the ancient CRT television flickered and froze as it attempted to entertain the three other drinkers in the bar with a tedious game of football; the glasses from which they drank their unidentifiable spirit looked more smeared than the backside of a diarrhetic camel. However, it was quiet, secluded and a convenient place to spend the rest of the day getting resoundingly hammered as one despaired about the state of the world and the fact that one was not being adored as a god.

"And who the hell do you think would make a spirit from fish?"

"Screw you," he muttered. "You know what I mean. Even the local alcohol has gone to pot."

"It's not like the old days," she agreed.

"It's not like the old days," he grumbled.

Ash poured two more shots of the definitely not piscine firewater. "Here's to how things used to be." They clinked their glasses and downed them. She set her glass back on the small, rickety table and was about to pour out some more when she looked up at her companion. He was sat staring straight ahead into nothingness. She waved her hand in front of his vacant face and got no reaction. "Ah well," she smiled. "More for me."

Then he started to scream.

This provoked concerned looks from the other drinkers in the bar. They were used to screams, especially from tourists who weren't used to the fiery alcohol that wasn't technically legal. However, the concern in their faces wasn't the screaming itself, it was the language in which it was screamed.

It wasn't human.

Panic gripped Ash as she, in turn, gripped Asmodeus. She shook his shoulders, desperate to stop the garbled mixture of angelic words that were spewing from his mouth. "Stop it!" she hissed. "What are you doing?"

Then his eyes snapped back into focus and held hers, exultation spreading his lips in a grin as tiny flames ignited in his dark, excited pupils.

"It's awake! It's awake!"

Ash was about to ask what was, when she noticed that the attention of the rest of the bar had turned to the archaic television. She frowned as she stood up and joined them in watching what seemed to be impossible. The football match had gone and had been replaced with some sort of news flash. It was footage of high up politicos and VIPs. They weren't doing what you would normally expect them to do: kiss babies, preach hatred and bile against their opponents, grin smugly at their acquired wealth. They were screaming in agony as they transformed into hideous wolf creatures before their features dissolved into a green mist and they fell down dead.

Asmodeus came and stood next to her, a beatific look on his face. "It's happening," he gasped. "It's finally happening. *The Bloodline shall die, the Harbinger shall burn, the Light shall waken. When these three things occur then you shall know that they who are one will battle and angels will walk the Earth,"* he recited.

Asherah could only stand and stare at the gruesome sights on the flickering screen. He was right. It was the first of the three signs of the Divergence: the death of the Bloodline of Abel, the cult of werewolves that had been obsessed with the Potency way back in the early years of Egypt.

"I can't feel it." Asmodeus was rambling to himself. "Well, I can *feel* it, but I can't *locate* it. It's not at full strength. I need to find it. I need it back in my hands."

Ash thought back to a small city in the North West of England, a dreary place that was normally cold and often wet. There was a man that lived there, a *curious* man. He did not react to her spell. When she sang, he did not fall under her mesmerisation. He was linked to all this, somehow.

"I know where it is," she said. "We need to go back to Lancaster."

Asmodeus' eyes burned bright as an understanding of her words sunk in.

"Spallucci," he growled.

"Spallucci," Asherah nodded, and after her companion left in an irate crack of static, she allowed herself a smile.

Things had just stopped being boring.

"Well, Samuel darling," she purred with the first true feeling of contentment that she had experienced in a very long time, "I hope you're ready for some guests." Then, letting her smile evolve into a fully-fledged grin, she clicked her fingers and vanished into thin air.

Two Left Feet

"Freddie!"

The ten-year-old boy just about heard his mum's call above the gratuitous sound effects of *Martian Squish 5*. He raced his reactive armour-avatar across the red killing field, pulse rifle in hand, splatting Martian brains left, right and centre as he called back the usual response: "Coming!"

"Well, make it quick, or tea will be cold."

A green-skinned boss rose up out of the red, alien planet surface and ripped off the head of Freddie's avatar, sending pixelated blood spraying up the screen. "*Fait accompli,*" he shrugged, switching off the console, although in his young head he saw the words as "Fate, a comm plea."

He swung off the bed and bounced down the stairs, the enticing aroma of his mum's Friday night pie reaching up and dragging him along by the nostrils. His stomach growled ravenously. "Smells good," he grinned as he entered the kitchen.

"Unlike this rubbish," his mum nodded towards the black bin bag by the back door. "Can you just bin it before we eat?" She started to bring the plates of food to the dining table.

"Sure thing." Freddie grabbed the bag and headed outside. The wheelie bin sat down behind the house, next to their car; he edged carefully past so as not to scratch the paintwork. He flipped up the lid of the bin, peered in and dumped the bag.

It was as he walked away that something odd struck him about the contents of the bin.

He turned, frowned and opened the black lid once more.

Shifting the black bag to one side, he stared down wide-eyed at the object that his rational brain had blocked out before his subconscious had given a polite cough.

It was a foot.

A human foot.

For a second, all he could do was just stand and stare at the severed piece of flesh that lay there, partially concealed, in a torn carrier bag. It had to be fake, obviously. For Heaven's sake, how could it not be? You just didn't find bits of bodies hidden in your rubbish. This was the real world, not the opening scene to a television detective show.

Freddie leaned in and pulled at the ripped bag then jumped back, the lid of the wheelie bin slamming shut. There had been a tattoo on the foot — a small red heart.

Just like the one on his mum's foot!

That was his mum's foot!

But, how could it be?

His mum was in the kitchen, serving up their Friday night pie, a concoction of the week's leftovers topped with a simple suet crust pastry. It was what she did every Friday, to make ends meet. What she *didn't* do was cut off her foot and dump it in the wheelie bin.

His mind raced. Had she been in possession of both her feet just now? Freddie was sure that he would have noticed. Surely she would have been somewhat lop-sided? Let's face it, being missing a foot would make walking around the kitchen whilst cooking tea rather awk-ward!

His heart leapt as his mother called out from the kitchen. "Tea's on the table!"

Freddie did the only thing that he could think of: he went inside, washed his hands and sat down at the dining table. He picked up his knife and fork and began to eat his pie. As he did, he couldn't stop himself from peering across the table at his mum. She seemed okay to him. She certainly didn't look like someone who had lost a foot. She was happily tucking into her own plate of food and chatting away about other grownups from work. She did this every night, and normally Freddie would just smile and nod in the appropriate places. In reality though, he didn't know who any of them were, but it seemed to make his mum happy to talk about them so he felt it would be very impolite to ignore her.

As she told him the apparently hilarious story of what one co-worker had said about another co-worker, Freddie carefully tried to peer under the table. Unfortu-nately, he was at the wrong angle, so had to gently scooch his chair over to the right just a bit. As he did, it scraped noisily on the tiled flooring.

His mum paused mid-tale. "You okay?"

The boy bolted upright. "Yep. Sure. Never better."

She smiled, shook her head and carried on with her story between mouthfuls of food.

Freddie chewed his bottom lip as he tried to fathom

a way to snatch a quick peek at his mum's feet. He looked at the gravy-smeared knife in his hand and had an idea. There was a clatter as it dropped to the hard floor.

"Freddie!"

"Sorry! I'll get it." He leapt down from his chair and bent down to retrieve the fallen cutlery. As he did so, he peered under the table. Across from him were the bare legs of his mother, poking out from under her tan-coloured skirt. At the end of them, in a small pair of pink slippers were both her feet. Freddie allowed himself a sigh of relief. It must have been a fake of some sort.

Then, just as he was about to stand up, he noticed something that caused him to squeak in worried excitement.

His mum's left foot was missing its tattoo.

He backed out from under the table, the knife still held in his hand.

"Freddie," his mum asked, "you okay?"

His mum.

His mum with a different foot.

That wasn't physically possible.

Which meant...

"You're not my mum," Freddie gasped, brandishing the knife in front of him.

The thing that looked like his mum frowned. "What do you mean?" it asked, imitating the voice of the woman who had loved him, cared for him. It lay down its knife and fork before rising from its seat.

Freddie backed away, the knife still out in front of him.

"You're not my mum," he repeated, hot tears welling out of his eyes. "You killed her and cut her up!"

The thing's face changed. It took on the look of

something that had been found out, like Sally Ferguson when people realised that she had wet herself at her eighth birthday party. "Freddie..." it began, but it was talking to empty space as the ten-year-old had fled from the kitchen.

He dashed through the hallway and out the front door. He had to get away. He had to clear his head and think about what he should do. Should he tell people? Not a chance, they would just think he was crazy. Imagine going to the police and saying that a stranger had walked into his house, cut up his mum and taken her place. They would say something like, "And how did you know it wasn't your mum?" to which he would reply, "Because her tattoo on her foot was missing," and they would then say, "But what about her face? Isn't that the same?" And to that he would have no answer, so they would either lock him up or call the thing that was pretending to be his mum, so either way he would end up miserable or dead.

He needed to go somewhere peaceful and quiet, somewhere he could make a plan.

He knew a perfect place.

The cemetery was empty. Technically it was closed, but Freddie was small and agile, so he was able to climb over the wall with relative ease. He sat on the grass and stared silently at the headstone. After an hour of sitting and staring, he still didn't have the slightest inkling of a plan.

If only his dad was still alive; he would have known what to do.

At least, Freddie presumed so. He had never known him. His dad had died when Freddie had been a babe in arms. All he really knew were the stories that his mum told him and the few pictures that he had of a brown-haired man holding a small infant.

Freddie sighed.

Then froze as he heard a footstep next to him.

"I thought I'd find you here," the thing that looked like his mum said.

Freddie scrambled to his feet and ran behind the gravestone, using it as a shield from the mum-murdering monster. "You killed her!" He screamed. "You killed my mum and took her face!"

The thing shook its head, a mockery of sadness on its stolen face. "No, Freddie. I *am* your mum. Trust me."

"I saw her foot! In the bin!"

The thing shrugged and sat itself down on the warm grass in the early summer evening. "I thought as much. I should have been more careful."

Tears streamed down the young boy's face. "So, you admit it. You killed her!"

"No. I truly am your mother." She patted the grass next to her. "Come here. I'll prove it."

Freddie stayed resolutely behind the protective headstone.

"When you were six, you accidentally sat on a lady-bird. You squashed it flat and cried for an hour.

"When you were four you convinced yourself that the newsreader on the telly was looking at you funny and would not sleep until I reassured you that he would not come and eat you in the night.

"If I'm not your mum, then how do I know those things?"

Freddie felt the first inkling of doubt edge its way into his mind. "But... the foot..."

The woman ran her fingers across the green, manicured graveyard grass. "Oh, how I've been dreading this day. I knew it would eventually come, but I had hoped to put it off until you were older."

"What do you mean?"

"Freddie, how did your dad die?"

"In a car crash. He was coming home late from work. A drunk ploughed into him. A hit and run."

The woman shook her head. "No, sweetie. There was no hit and run. There was a spaceship. *Our* spaceship.

"Your dad and I came to this planet twenty years ago. We settled down, blended in. We were very happy, especially when you came along. But then, we decided that it was time to move on. Things were getting ugly here. So your dad, he got the ship out of storage and prepped it for a test flight. It took off fine, but something went wrong. It lost power and crashed just out of town. Out by Hobson's field. You know the place?"

Freddie nodded as his mind reeled.

"It was dreadful. He managed to crawl out of the wreck, but the auto-destruct kicked in, vaporising the craft and throwing him across the road in the blast. He should have survived, if he had been left alone. If I had reached him before the emergency services, everything would have been all right. We regenerate, you see. Our wounds heal very quickly. But he dragged himself away from the crash site, trying to find a public phone box from which to ring me. Passersby found him and called an ambulance. Apparently he protested all the way to the hospital, but of course they didn't listen to him. They thought he was human.

"So they took him into the A&E and x-rayed him.

"They weren't to know that x-rays are lethal to us.

"I didn't even get to say goodbye.

"Anyway, this morning, just after you'd gone to school, I tripped over in the garden and snapped my wretched ankle. It was a stupid, fluke accident. I couldn't go to a hospital as the first thing they would want to have done would have been to x-ray me. So, I just lopped it off. Lord, it hurt like hell, but it grew back within a few hours."

Freddie walked cautiously around the side of the headstone. "You mean, I'm alien too?"

His mum nodded. "Sure are. I can prove it. She tossed him a sharp knife which she had pulled out of her handbag. "There you go. Just cut your little finger and watch what happens."

Freddie picked up the knife and looked at the sharp tip.

"Go on," the woman smiled reassuringly. "Just a quick nick."

He drew in a breath and slid the edge of the knife across his little finger, wincing as he did so. Then he looked on in fascination as the cut closed back up and knit seamlessly shut. It didn't leave the slightest trace of a mark.

Freddie thought back to all the times he had scraped his knees or bruised his arms. His mum would just clean him up, smile at him and say, "Good as new," as the cuts and bumps had miraculously healed or vanished under the careful application of a cold compress or a wad of cotton wool soaked in witch hazel.

"I thought, all the times I hurt myself, it was just down to you making me better," he said.

His mother smiled. "I suppose, in a way, it was. Your blood is my blood," she turned and looked at the gravestone, "and the blood of your father." She patted the ground next to her and pulled her tan-coloured skirt to one side, making room for her son.

Freddie walked over, sat down and curled up with his mum as they watched the alien sun setting on a planet that was hundreds of light-years away from their home.

Heart of Clay

They smell disgusting.

Look at them all: sacks of flesh and meat propped up with a fragile osseous structure. I used to think I was one of them, frail and feeble; weak; hormonal.

I know so much more now.

I am so much better than that.

I am the ultimate killing machine, hiding in plain sight.

They walk straight past me and they are none the wiser. They think I'm one of them, worrying about the things that concern them in their petty little lives: food, sustenance, sex, what to watch on the television whilst chowing down on that disgusting slop they call food.

I see the bigger picture now: the Divergence.

He will rise, my creator, and he will reduce this planet to ash. He will decimate its population, turning them into his vassals, his serfs. My kind will walk amongst them as lords, as kings. They shall look upon our true form and they shall cower in terror as we pass them by.

It will be glorious.

Oh, how I long for that day when the black dragon

shall spread his wings and claim all the treasure that is rightfully his.

That is the only hunger that I feel. Everything else is just an amusement to pass the time until I hear the voice of Kanor in my head and, for now, I wait amongst them, tasked with one labour: eliminate all those who might stand in my Maker's path.

Such as the Children of Cain.

I haven't encountered any of them yet, the vampires, but I know of them. It is programmed into my very structure, my being. They are the enemy of my Maker. They seek to prevent his glorious Divergence, and that cannot be allowed. Nothing must prevent that wonderful day, the day when my kin and I finally shed our human simulacra and respond to the call through time of our Lord and Master.

Just thinking about the vampires fans the flames within me that gives me life. The thought of extending my arm and plunging it through their chest. The bliss, the ecstasy.

But, for now, I will just practice on others around me.

Someone at random.

I will practice my skill, give in to my inner self.

Just as I did when I was reborn.

Just as I did to my family.

I thought that I was one of them. I believed that I had been born from a human womb, grown up with doting parents, then made my way into their world. I met my spouse three years ago in a bar. We had instantly clicked and soon made plans to spend the rest of our lives together. She already had kids and was worried that they might not take to me, see me as an interloper. But they loved me and I thought I loved them too. I would take them up to the park, play games with them: hide and seek, football, the usual mundane crap. I would buy them little gifts and feel delighted as they flung themselves around me for hugs and cuddles. They never suspected; *I* never suspected. I lived as one of them. I shared their lives, their stories, their food.

None of us knew that it was all a subterfuge.

None of us knew that I was a machine crafted to pass as one of them, able to complete the most basic of human tasks: physical, emotional, carnal.

Then the nightmares came.

I would be standing in a desolate land. The trees were ablaze and decaying bodies swung from their branches. The roads and towns were in ruins and the stench of decay hung in the air.

And I loved it all!

I would wake from these dreams sweating and con-fused. I would expect my breath to be short and my heart to be thumping. Yet there was neither of these things.

I found myself craving the night, the time when I would plunge down into the depths of this scorched world. I became distracted from the day-to-day. My new family bored me. I stopped going to work, annoyed and frus-trated with my banal colleagues.

My wife suggested that I seek help, counselling, and I told her that I would. But I never did. I would walk the streets and watch those around me with fascination. More and more they looked so totally *wrong* to me. Their heads seemed so small and their arms so short. They walked in a slovenly manner, as if they were made from jelly or grease.

Yet, I was the same. How could this be?

Then, one night, the dreams came again and I found myself stood with my true kin in our glorious Master's temple. There were rotten wooden seats, reminiscent of the building's former use as a parish church more than a thousand years previous. The air reeked of the decay from the damp wood and from the eviscerated cadavers that hung above us on a long wooden screen. He stood before us, his dark cloak around him and he lifted his arms into the air, speaking just one word:

"Awake."

And awake I did. In an instant I knew what I was. I saw my previous life as an embarrassing lie and my future as the liberating truth. I screamed as I was born anew and my arms reached out to embrace my real self.

I turned to my side in my nuptial bed and saw the look of horror on my wife's face. Her mouth was opening and shutting with no noise emerging from her lips. Her eyes were staring at my transformed arm that had plunged into her chest.

I sat, retracted my limb and looked down at the sharp stake that it had reflexively become. Her blood ran down its surface, rivulets of red tracking down to my elbow as her eyes glazed over in death.

I rose from our bed and made my way to the sleeping place of her children.

And that is how it has been for the last few months. I find subject after subject upon which to practice, to study. I befriend them, lure them away and dispatch them.

Sometimes I will reveal my true form to them, sometimes I just use a knife which I keep on myself all the time. It depends upon the situation; sometimes discretion is required, sometimes exhilarating brutality. Right now, I am trying to find a correct individual here in this place of freaks.

Even for humans, these must be the most pathetic. They are dressed as creatures from their fictions. Do they think that if they dress up like their heroes, they will stand any chance against their inevitable demise and death? Elves, aliens, robots: they are all here.

There is a man dressed as a Nordic god. He carries a plastic hammer as if it will bring down the elements upon his enemy. I could wrap my arm around his neck and suffocate him in a few seconds.

Over there is a girl showing far more skin than many in society would deem decent. What is she after? Attention? Gratification? A lance through her throat?

Then there is *that* guy. He wears a cheap *Star Trek* costume. His pointed ears are a poor fit and the black hair is obviously a wig. Look at him desperately trying to hand out leaflets for his pathetic comic book store to uninterested conventioneers.

But look, over there. That girl sits alone. She keeps fiddling with her phone. She is awaiting a call that will never come. She arranged to meet someone who has stood her up. I open my mouth and I can taste her despair. She wants to stay, *just in case*, but she knows the truth. She will be leaving here alone. Her eyes lift from the small device and scan the room, hoping that he or she will walk through the door. I shift my stance and it catches her eye.

I smile.

She smiles back.

I feel the weight of my knife against my side.

Yes, this one will do. She will walk away, sad and lonely. She will leave the convention and go stand above the bridge across the river behind the hotel where we are, and she will jump to her blessed release. At least, that is what people will think when they find her mangled corpse.

I put a step forward.

Then pause.

My insides churn as something else catches my attention. Something far more primal.

My eyes spy a short, dark-haired woman at the edge of the room and my skin flushes as her tantalising scent pirouettes on my tongue.

But she is no human. She is a vampire.

The pathetic little girl is forgotten. I turn and leave her to her disappointed misery.

At last, I have a worthy quarry.

This changes everything.

I Just Wish...

What the hell? I... I can't see! I can't see! My eyes... I can't open them.

Nonononono...

My arms! What's happened to my arms? I... I... can't...

My arms aren't there! No legs either.

I want to scream, but... No mouth.

Everything's so quiet; I can't hear anything. I can't smell anything either.

All I can do is feel something rubbing against me. It's cool and tickly. I think it's grass. It's rubbing against my skin.

Whoa, that's not skin. Whatever is rubbing against me is making a dry, scratchy sensation like I have a rough, hard surface. It feels familiar. It reminds me of little red spiders in the summer sun in my mum and dad's garden. There was an old wall next to the driveway. The spiders used to come out and scurry around on its patterned surface. They were hard to see as they were the same colour as the red grooves in the bricks that made up the wall. I'd run my small fingers over the cracked patterns and smile at the feel of the rough texture.

Jesus Christ, I'm a brick!

No. I can't be a brick. This is a dream, a nightmare. It's sleep paralysis. I used to get it when I was little. I'd have a stressful day when Mum and Dad were arguing. I'd go to bed and cry myself to sleep in a foetal position. I'd wish that my life was calm and quiet, that I would have nothing to worry about. But, instead, I'd dream that I was awake and I couldn't move, my arms and legs pinned together in that curled up position. I would feel like someone had crept into my room while I was sleeping and had covered me in superglue, binding my limbs tight together. My breathing would be hard and laboured and all I could feel was the rising panic in the pounding of my heart...

Oh. I've got no heartbeat.

I'm not breathing either.

Crap, I really am a brick.

How did this happen?

Why did this happen?

I want to cry, but I have no eyes.

I just have my memories.

Memories of Steve, of the life we had together. Our wonderful life.

Oh, Steve, you were always so good to me. I remember when you put in all those extra hours and got that bonus, so you bought me that vintage Porsche. Oh, God, I was over the moon. It was so beautiful: bright red and glinting in the sun. It was such a surprise. I know you'll find the time to teach me to drive sometime soon (well, if I'm not a brick and if this isn't some crazy nightmare), but I know you'll keep it ticking over for me, taking it on all those important business trips.

I just wish, perhaps, that you could have at least

helped me fill in that online form for my provisional licence.

But I know you love me very much. You're always telling me so. Especially when you get home from work. You work so very, very hard and buy me so many nice things. All the jewellery, the clothes and the perfume. You've spent so much money on our house too. I remember when you bought that sofa last month. It looks so great and fits you perfectly when you crash down into it when you get home and tell me that you love me and ask for a beer. I watch you as you doze off after tea. You look so adorable.

I just wish, perhaps, that you had paid me at least a little bit of attention after I'd cooked you such a nice meal.

And I know your work is hard and tiring, but it does have certain perks, like all those business trips abroad. I'd never been further than the Isle of Wight until I met you. Now I've travelled all over the globe: Malaga, Fuengirola, Marbella, Torremolinos. Such exotic places! I really enjoy lying by the pool, topping up my tan while you go and have your business meetings with the models that your company have asked you to assess. It's a shame that they leave you exhausted for the rest of the day, but you do work so very hard and have so many meetings. I really can't complain.

I just wish that, perhaps, those models hadn't been so pretty. A girl can't help but compare herself...

Oh, listen to me here, being so selfish. How could I possibly complain or whine about our idyllic little life together? Especially when you take me to so many parties. Oh, they are such fun! I get to have my hair and makeup done and put on a pretty little dress that you bought me especially for the occasion. I feel like a princess. I walk into the room on your arm and I see all those eyes turn towards us. It's like being royalty. You lead me over to a booth and buy me a large drink which will last me all evening then you go and mingle with your co-workers. Even then, you are working so hard to support me and give me everything I want, everything I need.

I just wish that, perhaps, you would come and sit with me for a few minutes.

Why is this making me feel so sad?

I can feel the cool grass brushing against my rough exterior. It's really rather soothing. Oh! Oh! The sun is rising. I can feel its heat on me. It's actually rather nice. It's calming.

There seems to be less to think about. Just the sensation of things around me. I just sit here, still and calm.

My mind feels clearer than it ever has been.

As the grass brushes against me and the sun warms me I feel like my memory is being polished, honed. I have no other external distractions. It's like looking into a muddy pool that is settling with the bottom becoming gradually clearer.

I really did enjoy watching those little red spiders on the bricks when I was a child. I would sit there for hours without moving, watching them scurry over their warm surface. I always wondered, as only a child can, what the bricks must be thinking. What did the bricks make of those little things hurrying around in relentless random patterns as they just sat there in their little wall, peaceful, not moving?

It always struck me that the bricks must have been far more content than the spiders.

Those tiny insects were always so busy, and for what? In a week or so they were gone, but the bricks remained. They stayed there all year, weathering the storms of winter and relishing the warmth of the summer. None of it mattered to the bricks; not the spiders, not the cold, not the heat. They took it all in their stride. No matter what the world threw at their rough, ridged surfaces, the bricks endured.

As my mum and dad did grown-up things such as arguing over money or complaining about work, I would sit there, next to that little red wall. I would wish and hope that someday I should have a life as simple and as uncomplicated as the bricks from which it was built. I longed for a life different to that of my parents; a life with nothing to worry about.

I remember when I left home to move in with you, Steve, thinking I had found that idyllic life, I walked out of my parents' house and down the drive. As I did, I happened to glance at the wall. It was exactly the same as it had been all those years ago when I was little. It had seen so much yet not been affected. Its red bricks had sensed all that had been around them, yet had remained unmoved.

They truly understood what they were and where they existed in the world.

Just as I do now.

I'm never going to drive that Porsche, am I, Steve? Let's be honest, you must have known that when you bought it. Who on earth would insure a new driver for something like that? You bought it for yourself, to make yourself look better with work.

I'm never going to get your full attention at home, am I, Steve? You just see me as a pretty little accessory who cooks and cleans and looks nice around the house. That's not really the way you should treat your partner, is it?

I'm never going to be the reason that we go on holiday, am I, Steve? No, you just take me because you don't know what else to do with me. So you dump me by the pool and swan off with some scantily-clad floozy to do God-knows-what. No wonder you're knackered all the time we're away.

I'm never going to get your attention at works' parties, am I, Steve? Why would I when you obviously have the reputation as the office stud? You swan in with a pretty little thing on your arm and dump her on her own with a large drink to butter her up then go and get off with a short skirt or big pair of boobs.

Oh dear.

When I was a little girl, I had those wishes that I would have a quiet life with nothing to worry about. I thought they had come true when I met you. I thought that I was being spoilt and provided for, but instead I was just something that belonged to you, a nonentity.

I remember last night when you came home in my Porsche (but it's yours, really). You smelt of expensive whiskey and slutty perfume. You collapsed into that sofa you bought for yourself and just fell asleep. As I watched you, I saw the red smear on your collar and I knew then that there would be no more holidays, no more parties. I went up to bed, undressed, curled up in the foetal position and wished again for a life where things were simple, uncomplicated, where I would have absolutely nothing at all to worry about, where I could just simply exist content, unworried.

And now as I feel the brushing of gentle grass, the

rhythm of a nearby brook and the caress of the warm sun-
shine, I know that, finally, my wish has been granted.

Through The Eyes of A Child

There was the sound of an almighty crash from the kitchen. This was followed by a long, violent curse in a string of words that had not been understood by human ears for over four millennia.

The slender blonde standing in the smart, fashionable living room allowed herself a knowing smile as she gazed out across the night-time cityscape down below, the artificial lights twinkling in the dark as she admired the view. Even now, after all these years, the continual advances in technology never ceased to amaze her. When she had been a child, darkness had been just that; complete and utter darkness. No one ventured out after nightfall except for thieves, vagabonds and whores. Now...

Now it was a twenty-four-hour world where no one ever seemed to sleep. More complicated times.

Her own species were, apparently, not quite so unique anymore.

She was aware of sotto voce muttering behind her as her long time life partner emerged from the kitchen war zone and now proceeded to fuss with and adjust the cutlery and crockery on the solid oak dining table. She turned and watched her red-headed companion move an errant knife first one way, then another before sighing, giving up and turning her ire on to a pepper pot that had dared to step out of line. Scorpion walked over, placed her cold hand on that of her love's and smiled.

"You think I'm worrying too much, Babe?"

Scorpion nodded.

Tigress gave another sigh. "It's just... I want it to be right, you know? After all she's been through."

The mute vampire nodded again. She knew exactly what Tigress meant. She squeezed the redhead's hand and gave another encouraging smile, accompanied by a nod.

Tigress glanced up at the over-ornate wall clock that hung next to the kitchen door. It was a tacky thing they had picked up in Egypt a couple of years ago and it was decorated with the seven ancient wonders of the world. It didn't really fit in with the clean, sleek lines of their fashionable penthouse suite but they had both agreed it brought back so many nice memories of their travels over the past couple of millennia. "They'll be here in ten minutes. You know they won't be late."

The "*they*" in question were their young queen, Nightingale, and her companion, the ever prompt Marcus. Nightingale had only recently ascended to the head of the Children of Cain after the traumatic events surrounding her brother's death a few months previous. Tigress and Scorpion, two of the oldest beings on the face of the planet, had watched as the petite female vampire had seemingly aged beyond her years as the weight of responsibility had begun to bear down upon her. They had decided that she deserved an evening of being spoilt and waited upon.

However, Scorpion sensed that the imminent arrival of their leader was not the sole cause of anxiety for her partner. There was something else bothering the normally carefree, party-loving redhead. She ran an affectionate finger down her lover's cheek, drew it around her perfect jaw bone and cupped the woman's delicate chin in her hand, drawing her face around so that their eyes were level.

"Scorp? What are you doing?"

The silent vampire just continued to gaze into the emerald eyes, searching out what was hiding behind them."

"Cassie..." Tigress' voice was quiet, nervous. "Don't you dare go all *prophetic* on me. Not tonight, of all nights."

Scorpion raised a blonde eyebrow. She only ever heard her old human name when her partner was worried or fretful.

"Damn it. I... I wanted to wait until the others were here. It's just... well, so much has happened, hasn't it? You know, with Justice and all that crap. Well, it makes you think.

"How much time do we have left?"

Scorpion frowned. She didn't like the sound of this. Not at all.

"No! No! Nothing like that! Gods no! Quite the opposite. We're funny things, aren't we? We're born knowing how we're going to die. We experience that final moment in our rebirth. But we never actually know *when*. It could be a few minutes after our heart stops beating or it could be centuries. Then, as we carry on in our new lives, we get carefree and careless. We think, because we've lived so long, that we are invincible, that nothing can touch us.

"But it can. And it's getting worse. There are more and more constructs out there. You know it. I know it. The others not so much. They've not been around as long as us. We've lived through so much more, from when humanity was a fraction of what it is now to this, when you can't turn around a corner without tripping over a distracted mortal as they gawp into their little mobiles.

"It's going to be dreadful when it happens, the Divergence.

"It's coming. I can feel it. One of these days we're going to turn a blind corner and there it'll be, not some sack of blood and bone playing on their latest gadget, trying to catch one of their little shiny creatures or attempting to line up god knows how many gems in a row, but we'll walk straight into an event of worldwide cataclysm. It'll be stood smiling, staring us right in the face and we'll never have seen it creep up and overtake us.

"And that scares me."

Scorpion smiled and stroked Tigress' cheek. She shook her head.

The other vampire held up a hand. "No, no, it's okay. It is. I know I'll survive Kanor's rise, at least for a while. We both know that we will.

"We've seen it.

"We know how it all ends for us.

"But there's just *so much!*" She ran her hand through her short red hair. "Ah, gods. How do you always do this? You say nothing, yet you get me to talk so much." She took a deep breath, placed her hands on either side of her partner's face and kissed her slowly on the lips. Then reached into the pocket of her tight jeans and pulled out a small box fashioned from a chestnut coloured wood.

"The thing is, we've been through so much and I know we're already a thing, we have been for over two thousand years, but I suppose, with all that's coming... I... I just want. Well, you know. You *always* know."

The redheaded vampire was for once, unable to find the words that she wanted, so instead she simply went down on one knee and opened the wooden box, revealing a small ring. It was gold and fashioned to look like ivy leaves plaited around a small, diamond that sparkled in the artificial light.

"Cassandra, will you make an honest if somewhat hot-headed, construct-slaughtering, night-dwelling creature out of me?"

Then everything turned grey...

Scorpion blinked and the grey began to fade. She was no longer standing in her home and she was no longer with Tigress.

Where the hell was she?

As the grey dissipated, she saw that she was stood in a bedroom, but certainly not one that looked suitable for sleeping in. The large, king-size bed had been rammed up against the door as an impromptu barricade, and its occupant, a middle-aged man in a crumpled grey suit was backed up into a corner, gibbering to himself as tears of abject terror flowed down his cheeks.

Scorpion made to move towards him but found that her feet were immobile, stuck in one spot.

Okay, she thought to herself. *Let's see what happens then.*

It was then that she smelt it. The wolf, the member of the Bloodline of Abel.

Her blue eyes snapped up to a Velux window in the

ceiling of the room. A huge, clawed paw eased the window out of its frame and a sandy-haired beast dropped down into the chaos of the room. The cowering man began to scream in a manner that strongly suggested all sanity had departed his broken mind as the werewolf purposefully strode over towards him. The beast silenced the screams by grasping the man around the neck and squeezing forcefully.

Then it proceeded to make him suffer.

All the while, Scorpion stood and watched, unable to intervene. Every nerve in her body wanted to lunge forward and protect the human from the member of the Bloodline yet, try as she may, she could not move from her corner of the bedroom as blood, viscera and bone were strewn around her.

Eventually, when the man was no more than a pile of bleeding detritus, the werewolf stopped and carefully arranged the decapitated head on the dressing table. It reached into the dead mouth and ripped out the tongue, which it chewed to a paste then spat out. As it placed the masticated organ next to the head, everything turned grey once more.

The next room was a stark contrast to the previous one.

Scorpion found herself stood in the shadows of what looked like a penthouse office. A wide, panoramic window gazed out across a skyline that felt somewhat familiar. In front of the nighttime vista stood two lifelike, incredibly detailed statues: Anubis and Orion. Her stomach lurched. More Bloodline.

As the grey dissolved, she became aware of two more men. One she did not recognise. He was the epitome of what modern society regarded as handsome: tall and blonde, muscular and wealthy. However, as his pervading scent reached her nostrils, she could immediately smell what he *truly* was, beneath the human façade, and her hackles rose.

The other man she knew in an instant.

Spallucci was stood pointing a revolver at the wolf in man's clothing. The two of them were talking but the words were spoken as if through water; distorted and unintelligible. Then the gun roared into life and a red flower blossomed on the rich man's perfect white shirt. He said something as he stared in disbelief at the mortal wound before Spallucci stepped forward and blew his handsome face across the plate glass window.

Everything froze. She gazed in wonder at the smoke rising from the muzzle of the gun, the detailed patterns on the glass from the sprays of blood, bone and brain, a small vein pulsing in the right temple below Spallucci's dishevelled curls.

Scorpion felt a dread chill slither through her veins.

"I didn't like him at all," came a child's voice. "He got what he deserved."

The vampire looked down as a small girl walked into view, but not the sort of girl that you saw every day walking down the streets or heading to school, idly gossiping to her mates. This one's hair was long and green and her eyes burnt like emeralds, a wispy haze drifting up from them. Her dress was long and white, flowing down to her bare feet which now stood before the deceased member of the Bloodline. She peered up at the mangled remains of the wolf's head and frowned. Slowly, she levitated off the plushly carpeted floor, her white dress flowing around her. When her face was level with that of the gunshot victim, she leant forward and appeared to study it in the manner that a collector would study a recently gassed butterfly. "Definitely dead," she surmised. "Just one more to go." She glided down to the stained carpet with no apparent effort, turned to Scorpion and cocked her head to one side.

The vampire felt as if she had another being rummaging around inside of her. She struggled and strained but still could not move. Baring her fangs, she hissed at the weird child.

The little girl just clapped her hands with glee. "Oh, I like you! You know my mummy! She talks to you."

Scorpion's brow creased in confusion as she tried to understand what it was that the weirdling was yammering on about. Then she was aware of a noise just at the edge of her senses. It was a vibrating whisper that made the fine hair on her arms stand on end in a primal response.

The girl clapped her hands together in obvious glee. "That's it! That's it! You can hear her, can't you?" Then, closing her green eyes, she swayed rhythmically to and fro as she hummed a three note refrain over and over.

Scorpion felt the invisible force that had been holding her relinquish its grasp. She rubbed at the hairs on her arms and took a tentative step towards the strange child. The room was filling with grey smoke once more, Spallucci fading away into nothing as he ran out of the penthouse, leaving the blasted remains of the werewolf behind him.

"Can you hear it? Can you hear it?" asked the child, her face fixed in a beatific smile. "Such a beautiful song."

Scorpion strained to try and focus on the words that

were just out of earshot. She shook her head.

The girl opened her eyes and they blazed a bright emerald green as the smoke enveloped them both. "Then you have more to see..."

The stench of dank reached Scorpion's acute sense of smell even before the fog cleared. She wrinkled her nose at the offensive odour. As the clouds thinned, she saw the source of the smell. She, and the small girl, were stood at the edge of another room. This one was part of what appeared to be a derelict warehouse. The room was large and in a terrible state of repair. Whitewash was peeling from damp walls, wooden shutters hung rotten in their casements, providing a feeble attempt at keeping out the sun. The flooring was chipped and warped, with occasional floorboards missing.

It was quite apparent that this property had not been used for its intended purpose in a very long time.

However, it was occupied right now.

There were two beings here. One was a blonde teenage girl. She was curled up against a far wall, her knees pulled up tight to her chest as if she were trying to make herself as small as possible, invisible. The other person was an adult, and that was all that Scorpion could tell from looking at them. They stood tall in the middle of the room, but were completely unidentifiable due to the way that they were attired. Their long, tattered and stained coat covered a body that was swathed in rags. It was not possible to see the slightest square millimetre of their skin. Even their face was bandaged tight, with a pair of dark glasses wrapped firmly into place in front of their eyes. *He looks like the Invisible Man on crack*: Scorpion thought to herself.

She breathed in, trying to discern what manner of creature this was, but the overpowering stench from the building and from the very rags that the being wore made that impossible.

However, there was something familiar about the individual, about the way they stood: tall, erect.

"Yes," came the voice of the weirdling. "You know him. You know him very well."

And then it struck her. She thought back to their visitors who were due this evening; to Marcus, tall, determined, rigid. Her eyes slipped back to the blonde girl and Scorpion's hand flew to her mouth in realisation.

"Yes!" cried the child. "Yes! Now you see it. Now you know."

Scorpion shook her head as tears of blood began to trickle down her cheeks. She ran to her friend, swathed in rags, and tried to reach out to him, to hold him, but her insubstantial hands just passed straight through his rag-adorned body. The whispering voice that was just beyond her hearing increased somewhat in volume and she could start to make out snatches of words: "Bloodline... Harbinger..." She looked over to the green-haired child, her eyes pleading.

"You know this cannot be changed," it explained. "He has already seen his fate."

The vampire slipped her hands up under her long hair and laced her fingers together at the nape of her neck. She shook her head again in frustration. She could not see this. She could not bear it.

"Do not be sad," said the child. "All things die. All things end. This is just his time."

Scorpion came and stood next to her, tears now flowing freely, the heel of her hand absent-mindedly rubbing the crimson streaks away from her cheeks. Marcus was pacing around the warehouse. He appeared to be talking, explaining something to the terrified girl but, as with Spallucci, Scorpion could not make out the words. All she could hear were scratchy whispers that were crawling through her brain, repeating the same words over and over: "Bloodline... Harbinger..."

As she watched, something about Marcus became clearly apparent.

The poor vampire had lost his mind. Something had broken him.

His movements were jerky, erratic as he continued to pace, to prowl around the room. Every now and then he would stop, pause as if listening to an internal voice, then reply first to that then to the girl that was still sat cowering by the wall.

Then, eventually, he stood motionless, a certain calm fallen over him.

He nodded, either to himself or to the internal voice of which only he was conscious, and turned to face a large pair of wooden doors at the far end of the warehouse. His hands went up to his face, his fingers exploring the cloths that covered him, probing at their tattered edges, as if only just realising that they were there.

Scorpion couldn't watch, didn't want to watch, as she knew what was to follow.

But she knew she had to.

She watched as her old friend said something to the girl that caused the teenager to look up at him.

She watched as he walked to the far end of the room and swung open the battered doors, allowing bright sunlight to flood inside.

She watched as slowly, methodically he unwrapped the foul-smelling bandages from around his face, revealing a visage that was overflowing with beatific grace.

She watched as he stepped out into the harsh light of day.

She watched as he spread his arms to accept the sun and subsequently burst into flame.

She watched as passersby gasped in horror before they fished out their phones and started to snap photos and video, fresh for social media.

She watched as everything, once more, turned to grey.

As the mist began to clear, the distraught vampire found that she was crouched down on the floor, her hands beating at the ground. She wept freely for her dead friend. Yes, death was inevitable, but it was so painful to watch the passing of one you loved.

"He accepted it," came the voice of the weird child from behind her as Scorpion felt a small comforting hand stroke her back. "You must not mourn him. You should celebrate his action. Did you not see the look on his face? That was not one of sorrow. It was joy."

Scorpion took a deep breath and pulled herself up onto her haunches.

She glowered at the child.

She was not feeling joyful, not one little bit, and still the nearly imperceptible words were tapping at her subconscious: "Bloodline... Harbinger... Bloodline... Harbinger... Bloodline... Harbinger...

"Light!"

Scorpion gasped as the third word resonated through her head. It was as if the entire universe had bent down and screamed in her ear. She sprung to her feet and saw the small girl scream with glee and run off into the parting mist as she cried out, "He's here! He's here!"

The vampire shook her head and pursued the weirdling. As she did, she started to take in their new surroundings. They were in what appeared to be a small suburban garden, but not one that was either loved or cared for. Scorpion noted that the grass was poorly cut, with a rusted, abandoned lawnmower propped up against the wall of a redbrick house. Elderly rose bushes stood overgrown and unpruned in untended borders that were choked with dandelions and couch grass. Bulging bags of rubbish had been unceremoniously dumped by a broken garden gate and a quick sniff told her that they were full of empty beer cans. A couple of plastic garden chairs and an old barbecue sat on a patio that was overrun with insidious weeds crawling up from the ragged gaps between the mismatched paving slabs.

The child halted by one of the chairs and clapped her hands together with glee as the back door to the suburban house banged open. Scorpion found herself holding her breath. What manner of individual could bring such excitement from the bizarre child?

As the occupant of the house emerged through the door, she found herself decidedly underwhelmed.

He was middle-aged, unkempt and rather overweight.

This, however, did not diminish the excitement of her odd little companion. "We're going to have such fun!" she squealed as she hopped from foot to foot, following the man who was hefting an old portable television out into the garden. It was plugged into a frayed extension cable that fought back against his efforts, continually tangling itself up as he unreeled it on his way over to the chairs. "So much fun," she repeated, her emerald eyes blazing bright. "They will rise to your command, yes they will. From the earth they shall be born and they will march. March into battle."

Scorpion approached the overweight man and winced as he bent over, exposing far too much bum cleavage whilst setting the television up on one of the chairs. As it flickered into life, he eased himself down into the other chair and cracked open a beer which he fished out of a cooler that sat on the patio.

The vampire looked at the man then at the child. What on earth was she not seeing here? She sniffed the air around him, but all she was rewarded with was the scent of economy-priced alcohol and the body odour of the terminally obese.

He was watching something trashy on the television. A man in a suit and a smarmy smile was encouraging a young couple to shout at each other. The man was nodding in appreciation. He really seemed to be enjoying the trashy daytime show.

Doesn't look like he does much else: Scorpion observed. She lay a hand on the child and frowned as it turned to smile up at her.

"Isn't he wonderful?" the girl gasped. "So much... power! We will do great things together."

Scorpion frowned. This was getting rather disturbing.

"Oh," the child giggled, covering her mouth with a tiny hand. "I see. You don't see him, do you? Not properly. Not yet. I forget that you just walk a single path. It must be so confusing for you."

The *definitely* confused vampire just shrugged.

"Don't worry. It will become clear. Watch." She pointed to the television as the flickering image changed. Gone were the arguing couple. They were replaced by a reporter speaking in an intense, hurried manner from an "*on the scene*" location to the audience at home via a handheld camera.

Scorpion felt her stomach lurch as she saw a familiar pair of old wooden doors in the rear of the shot. Suddenly the warehouse doors flew open and an individual walked out between them. He was swathed in ragged bandages. The camera zoomed in on him, hungry for a prize-winning report. Scorpion stood transfixed as the man began to unwrap the rags from around his face and the scene unfolded once more of Marcus greeting the sun for the final time.

She snatched her eyes away from the set, unable to witness the death of her friend once more. Instead she found herself watching the man in the garden chair. His eyes were locked on the events unfolding on the television

Eyes that burned with raging fire.

Scorpion gasped as she felt something immeasurable sweep over her, making her feel like the smallest, most insignificant atom in all of creation.

"Yes!" cried the child. "Now you truly see him. Now you feel his unstoppable power."

And she surely did. No longer was she stood in the rundown back garden of an insignificant suburban house but she was soaring high up in the sky, above the vast entirety of all Creation itself and a being stood there, his entire form ablaze with the brightest flame that she had ever witnessed. In his fiery hands he held two objects: a chalice and a sword, the Cup and the Blade, the two

Eternals that her kind had been tasked with seeking out. Around him swept a crazed maelstrom as he reached out with the Blade and pierced the very fabric of the night sky. Scorpion listened as the child sang out in joy, the same three note melody she had heard before and, in return, this tune was echoed from the watery liquid that poured out of the wound in the fabric of space. The wound opened wider and wider, swallowing the stars and galaxies as it did, effortlessly dragging them down into its widening maw, the melody growing louder and louder.

She watched as the being of pure Light moved its mouth in time to the song whilst the dying reality was swept up by the incoming Abyss and gathered up in the bowl of the Cup.

"We are one... We are one... We are one..."

Then, with an equal mixture of awe and terror, Scorpion watched as the last remnant of Creation was drawn up into the Cup and the living sea enfolded itself around the three beings that remained: the Cup, the Blade, the Light. A pulsing green glow drifted toward them and coalesced into the form of another girl, identical to the one that had accompanied her. Her companion smiled. "I have to leave you now. It's been fun. We'll play again another time." Then, taking the hand of her sister, they were absorbed into the fabric of the singing sea.

Scorpion closed her eyes as the words of the Abyss touched her lips once more.

"The Bloodline shall die, the Harbinger shall burn, the Light shall waken. When these three things occur then you shall know that they who are one will battle and angels will walk the Earth."

"Cassie! Cassie! You okay?"

"She's coming round."

"I can see that. Cassie, sweetie, can you hear me?"

Scorpion opened her eyes and felt a hoarseness to her vocal cords. She reached up with an uncertain hand, grimaced and rubbed at her throat.

"Yeah, Babe," came Tigress' concerned voice. "It happened again. You remember much?"

Scorpion felt a strong pair of hands lifting her up from the hard floor. She saw a concerned pair of grey eyes looking at her over an impeccably neat moustache. She flung herself forward and wrapped her arms tight around Marcus' neck, desperate to eradicate from her memory all that she had just witnessed. She felt a perplexed hand gently patting her on the back and she pulled back. Gazing into his honest eyes, she smiled sadly.

"Scorpion, what did you see?"

She turned and saw the owner of the third voice. Her queen, Nightingale.

"The words you spoke. Do you understand them?"

The three words echoed around inside her head once more: "Bloodline... Harbinger... Light..." She nodded.

"What's going to happen?"

Scorpion said nothing. She just looked again at the male vampire, tears welling up in her eyes; sorrow that she could not contain.

Marcus just nodded.

Then something hit her. Something intangible. The others drew in a sharp breath and she saw it had touched them too.

"What the hell was that?" Tigress growled.

Scorpion walked over to the large television that hung on their wall. As she switched it on, she was sure that she had heard the sound of a small girl laughing. A news item was playing and what she saw caused her to sink down into their sofa as all strength left her legs. Something inexplicable was happening around the planet. Across the globe, individuals, most of them in positions of power or influence had screamed out in agony as they had apparently transformed into wolves then dropped down dead.

"*The Bloodline shall die...*" Nightingale whispered as she too sat down on the sofa, her hand raised to her mouth in astonishment. "Good God, can it be...?"

"How?" Marcus asked.

Scorpion thought back to the scene in the penthouse, a werewolf having its brains used as a window decoration. "*Just one more to go,*" the weirdling had said.

She reached for a notepad and pen that she kept on their coffee table and, as the others watched her, scribbled one word down which she turned round to show them:

Sam.

A Late Night Drink

He knew that evening was gonna be a bad one.

Roger was no psychic, just your run of the mill simple, straight-laced barman; but anyone who does their job properly knows when things are gonna go pear-shaped.

This was one of those nights.

First there was the TV. It was one of those big wi-descreen jobs. The *Plasmatron 2000* the locals joked. The brewery had insisted on its presence.

"Our focus groups say that football is now a major player in the leisure industry," the memo had been worded.

Great, Roger had thought as he had struggled to mount it to the wall, armed only with a rusty drill and a Phillips screwdriver. *I wonder if hernias are major players too?*

But, give it its due, punters had come more often and drunk more steadily since the installation of the *Plasmatron 2000*. So Roger couldn't really complain *too* much.

Until tonight.

The thingy-box had died. The black rectangle with the flashing lights and the three antennae that lived under the bar, connecting the obscenely large television to a universe of football, rugby and other untold sporting delights.

At least, Roger surmised it had died. One minute, twenty-two overpaid blokes in shorts had been kicking a ball up and down an immaculate patch of grass, the next, some sort of horror film had come on.

He tried changing the channel, but the damned film seemed to be on every single one, so the thingy-box must have definitely died.

Not knowing what else to do, Roger had just left the film running. *Perhaps*, he thought to himself as he watched the movie, *the thingy-box is having a little kip, like old man Gardner normally does after his seventh pint. It might wake up in a bit and start asking for peanuts.*

Truth be told, it was a rather weird movie. There was some guy in a mask dressed up as a wolfman. He was howling and screaming lots, so Roger had muted the sound.

Now, Roger was no Philistine. He knew in his heart of hearts that sure this pic must be a classic. It was the wolfman after all and he was up there with Dracula and Frankenstein. However, he reckoned that this must be some weird-assed modern adaptation. For starters, it was in colour, not black and white. All the classics were in black and white. Secondly, it just seemed to be a variation of the same shot of this guy howling and screaming as he changed from human to wolf. It was the same effect over and over, set in different locations. True, he had to hand it to the guys who'd done the CGI, it looked damned realistic, especially that weird green stuff that kept oozing out of him, whatever that was supposed to be. But it felt somewhat monotonous. It reminded him of the time his sister's lad had made that video for his BTEC film studies course about the life of a dandelion.

Roger sighed. There was no accounting for taste these days. Plus, at the end of the day, horror flicks don't sell beers as well as footie. As a result there were just the three hardened regs in, drinking until they inevitably dropped.

Only, tonight, they weren't just drinking. They were also bitching.

And guess what about?

Yeah. The lack of football.

Roger wouldn't have minded so much, but these guys never even watched the blessed thing. All night long they just sit and sup, sit and sup.

But no, tonight it was sit, sup, bitch; sit, sup, bitch.

Just the three of them.

That was until his second problem walked in.

He was young. And wet. Yeah, Roger observed, very wet. It was pissing it down that night. Had been for about the last half hour. He felt kind of sorry for the kid, must have been cold and drenched, but the law was the law and he did not want his ass kicked when the police took his licence away.

Knowing that the kid must be underage, he asked for ID.

Yeah, he was sure he had asked for ID. Must have done.

You don't need to see my identification.

Where had he heard that before? It was gonna bug him all night. A film? TV?

Anyway, he asked the kid what he wanted to drink.

The kid fixed his blue eyes on a bottle of Jack Daniel's and nodded.

"The bottle, please."

Roger got it down off the shelf and set it down with a tumbler.

Then, well he had the strangest feeling that the kid had already paid him. So he hovered about a bit, smiling a slightly stupid smile, before deciding it would be best to busy himself polishing some glasses over by his regulars.

"Hey, Roger! Where's the bloody footie then?"

"You know the thingy-box is screwed, John. I've told you that twice already."

"Oh," muttered the drinker, returning to his pint.

"Thingy-box…" pondered the guy next to him, holding a glass of Guinness halfway up to his mouth. "I'm sure my son has one of those."

John looked at him, "Your son? I never knew you were rich mate! Who gives a kid a thingy-box?"

The Guinness drinker shook his head, "S'only a little thing. Uses it with those plastic monsters he's got. Digithingies or something, they're called. You know the ones."

John and the other drinker just looked at him blankly.

"Didn't know you could use it with the TV, though. Mind you, I never tried."

"Pete," said the third drinker, "You're pissed."

"Screw you, Mike," hit back Pete. "When will it be fixed, Roger?"

Roger shrugged.

"So, for now, it's old Fuzz Face in the mask up there?" John commented.

"Yup, old Fuzz Face." Pete looked up at the flick on

the box, then raised his pint of Guinness, "God bless 'im an' all who sail in 'im!"

"Gotta feel sorry for him I s'pose," said Mike.

Pete: "And why's that, then?"

"Well, it ain't his fault he's an ugly bugger."

They chuckled.

"And there was me thinking he just didn't shave this morning," Pete was actually going a bit red in the face now. From laughter or alcohol, it was hard to tell.

"Nah, seriously," continued Mike, "I've seen this before. It was a curse or summat. Turned him into old Wolfie up there. Poor fella can't help but kill people. He don't wanna do it. He just does, you know."

Roger, who was now wiping up various spills from gesticulated glasses, noticed that the young lad (who had already drunk about half of the Jack Daniel's bottle) was listening quite intently to the discussion even though he was still facing away. There was just the odd sidelong glance that only barmen could notice.

John regarded the wolfman with some scepticism, "Don't look that hard to me. Bet I could teach him a thing or two. Spends so much time ravishing virgins, bet he don't even know the Queensbury rules." At this, he set his near-empty glass down on the bar and got up off his stool, albeit rather unsteadily. "I'd teach him a thing or two." Then, rolling his sleeves up, he proceeded to shadow box around the bar.

His drinking companions were now in hysterics at the sight of their drunken friend doing a very bad impression of Ali or Fury.

But even through the raucous laughter, a quiet voice stopped them dead.

"You would have been dead before you got down

off your stool."

The laughing stuttered to a halt. The drinkers and Roger turned to look at the boy. He had just downed another bourbon and was looking straight ahead into the mirror behind the bar.

"Excuse me?" John wasn't even sure that it was the boy that had spoken, but it had to be. Apart from Roger and the three of them, there was no one else in the bar.

The boy turned on the barstool and levelled his pale blue eyes at them. "By the time you had moved to put your first foot down on the floor, a werewolf would have torn your throat open and broken your backbone, immobilising you. It would then proceed to drag you away before ripping your guts open, feeding on your intestines and stomach first, before moving on to your other organs. And don't believe it's a mercy killing, either. They like you to suffer. You will feel every last little bite as you are consumed mouthful by mouthful. Bit by bit."

The three regulars normally had an answer for everything, but to this they had none.

Mike began to open his mouth but the boy cut in, "And don't believe that crap about a curse. I've not yet met a werewolf who hasn't loved it. They thrive on the power. It consumes them and drives them on. They give in to the dark side of their soul and let it push them onwards and upwards to places you could never even dream of travelling. They never fight the all-consuming rage. They never mourn those they murder. They just devour anyone who stands in their way."

Roger felt he must do something. "Now, come on lad," he said, "The guys are only just enjoying a pint and the movie. There's no need to get all serious like that, is there?"

But, when he looked into those blue eyes he knew that this *was* the time to get serious. *Very* serious indeed.

They expected more. They really expected him to say more. Roger, cloth in hand. Mike and Pete with their pint glasses. John with his sleeves rolled up to his elbows.

But he didn't. He shook his head, picked up the half-empty bottle of bourbon and walked back out into the rainy night.

John turned and sat back down on his stool. The four of them looked at each other. Then a group enlightenment seemed to spread across their faces.

Pete voiced the group's thought. "Did he say that he'd *met* a werewolf?"

Author's Notes

Many thanks for buying this, my latest little anthology of stories. I hope you enjoyed both the stand-alones and those which dipped their toes into the ever-expanding waters of the Spallucciverse. Here are a few little things you might like to know about the tales you've just read.

How The Tibbles Got His Name.

Whenever I go to events and I'm asked to read one of my short stories, I normally pull out *Needs Must* from *All Things Dark And Dangerous* as it has consistently remained my favourite of all my little works, telling the tale of Odd Bod as he climbs out of his well. I have a feeling that his reign may have come to an end with this little gem. On the surface of it, *Tibbles* starts off as a charming tale of a small girl who likes to dress up as knights and green men rather than Disney princesses. However, as the story progresses, my more eagle-eyed constant readers will start to notice small details cropping in from the wider Spallucciverse and we start to realise that she is in fact a major player in that world, albeit just in her infancy.

It was an absolute joy to write and I smile every

time that I read it back. I hope you will too.

Awakening.

In *Sam Spallucci: Bloodline*, DCI Jitendra Patel refers to an incident in the Middle East that led to Vincent Stone getting his hands on half of the Potency. This short story is that event in greater detail. I originally wrote it as I drafted the conversation between Sam and Jitendra, having both documents open at the same time and tweaking each one as they simultaneously progressed. Then, after introducing the human avatar of the Potency in *Bloodline* (and, I must add, having a hoot working with her), I went back to *Awakening* and added her down in the dig site.

As is heavily suggested in this short, I am not yet finished with the unnamed protagonist. He will have a major, cataclysmic role to play in the forthcoming novel *Fallen Angel*, so watch this space for that one.

Aside from the fantasy world in which the story is set, the problem of illegal antiquities in Israel and the surrounding area is a serious matter. Artefacts can literally be found just under the ground, leading to unauthorised digs springing up and historical sites being ransacked and destroyed before museums and universities get there, leading to very prestigious finds ending up in the hands of private collectors rather than in the public domain. As far as I am aware, none of these collectors are actually werewolves, but I may be wrong. Who knows for sure…?

6:25

The first story in this anthology that isn't set in the Spallucciverse is based around that horrific occurrence that I am sure many of us have experienced at one time or another: waking from a dream only to realise we are still dreaming. This used to happen to me a lot when I was younger and always left me totally disorientated, normally for the rest of the morning. I decided to take this idea, run with it, and turn it into something even bigger.

Let Sleeping Dragons Lie.

So, this is the third and final journey into the Dragon storyline (the previous two appearing in my last two anthologies *Mourning Has Broken* and *Hide Not Thou Thy Face*). There is so much that I want to say about this one, but I have to be careful as that way spoilers lie. All I will say is, go back and reread Sam's adventures, looking carefully at prophecies that have been mentioned (especially ones concerning dragons). Also, there is a scene in *Songbird* where the young Esther encounters Sophia/Eloise in All Saints which is well worth studying for tasty little tidbits.

I would be very curious to hear as to who my readers think the protagonist of these stories is and what his future will hold. The answer might not be as simple as it at first appears. All I will say is that he is someone major in the Spallucciverse and that we have already met him numerous times.

Priorities

This is my little piece of flash fiction for the anthology. People who know me know that my mind constantly flits from one thing to the other, normally from the mundane to the surreal and vice versa. I kind of feel that this story would be me to a tee should I suddenly flip and kill someone.

Relics

The fourth story here in the Spallucciverse picks up where *Awakening* left off. We last encountered Asherah and Asmodeus in the short story *Second Time Around* in the anthology *All Things Dark And Dangerous* where Ash we eternally bored with a lifetime on Earth and seriously starting to regret her decision to leave Heaven.

In *Relics,* we have moved on a few months and see that her ennui still has a full hold on her. She longs for the old days where she was worshipped as a goddess, yet she feels that something destructive is looming on the horizon. The story ends with the climactic events of *Sam Spallucci: Bloodline*, leading nicely into the next outing for Sam *Fury of the Fallen*.

Two Left Feet

I've said it before, and I'll say it again, I am a huge fan of Philip K Dick, especially his short stories. Just before I started work on this anthology I had read his short *The Father-Thing* which was adapted into a screenplay for *Philip K Dick's Electric Dreams* back in 2017. *Two Left Feet* is my little homage to this story, albeit going down a less dark avenue.

Heart of Clay

So, this short from the Spallucciverse is going right back to *The Case of the Vexed Vampire* and the *Nightingale* short story. Here we see the build-up to the events of Dave Nichol's turning through the eyes of the construct that Nightingale and Marcus were chasing. I even included a cameo glimpse of Dave himself in the story.

I think I just wanted to show, once and for all, that there is no hope for constructs, that they are pure killing machines and totally irredeemable. But, then again, that might all change in the Bobby Normal novellas…

I Just Wish

As well as being an author, I'm also a private tutor and, last year, I was trying to tease some creative writing out of one of my students who found the process some-what burdensome. We were bouncing around ideas and the ones that she came up with were all rather mundane and day-to-day. Then, out of nowhere, I suggested, "What if your protagonist woke up one day and was a brick?"

She may not have used the idea, but I certainly wasn't going to let it go.

Through The Eyes of a Child

The second prologue in this anthology to *Sam Spallucci: Fury of the Fallen* takes us back to the world of the vampires, the Children of Cain. I absolutely adore Scorpion and Tigress; they remain two of my favourite characters in my books. Here we get a glimpse into how their millennia-long relationship is entering new territory just before another prophecy hits Scorp square in the face, leading us, as does *Relics*, into the next chapter for Sam.

All I will say right now is *Fury of the Fallen* will be a blast and as for the climactic scene… Well, just wait and see.

A Late Night Drink

A curious little addition this one, serving as it does as an epilogue to *Sam Spallucci: Bloodline*. Originally, way back in the dim and distant past, *Bloodline* was inten-ded to be the last Sam Spallucci book and, due to the way that it was supposed to end, it was going to be told in the third person rather than through the first person noir that is Sam's usual style. We were to see, through the eyes of Alec his lodger, Sam's world being torn apart. *Drink*, in its original format, was intended to be part of a threefold pro-logue which would also include Stone becoming a were-wolf (now the short story *Orion's Child*) and a scene where someone close to Sam discovered they had a ter-minal illness (this was, instead, worked into the whole series as an unfolding thread).

Anyway, the world of Lancaster's paranormal in-vestigator grew far larger than I had originally intended, meaning that *Bloodline* would actually be towards the middle of the timeline rather than at the end. Also, the idea of third-party storytelling really sucked, so it stayed as first person.

However, I still had this little scene kicking around with Alec reflecting on the traumatic events of the story. I felt it worked and it was nice to give Alec some quality scene time, so to speak. As a result, it transformed into the story that we now have.

ASC 2022

About The Author

A.S.Chambers resides in Lancaster, England. He lives a fairly simple life of walking in the countryside, gazing at mountains and wondering if clouds taste of candy-floss.

He is quite happy for, and in fact would encourage, you to follow him on Facebook, Instagram X, TikTok, Patreon and YouTube.

There is also a nice, shiny website:
www.aschambers.co.uk

9 781915 679376